Garland glanced up at the sky. "It's really beautiful out here. I love nights like this when the moon is full."

Ryker just sat there absorbing what she'd said.

Garland gave him a sidelong glance. "This is such a perfect night."

He pulled her to her feet. "You're right," he murmured. "Everything about this night is perfect."

Ryker backed her up until her legs hit the poolside table and she stood pressed up against the hard surface. There was no escape.

Garland's breath quickened, making her breasts rise and fall faster as they brushed against his chest. Her cheeks were flushed, and her lips were swollen from his kisses.

It was clear that Garland wanted him, but she was fighting herself as much as she was fighting him.

Ryker did not just want her. He needed her.

He felt a low growl rumble in his throat, and then he crushed his lips against hers. Grabbing her neck to pull her closer, he pushed his tongue against her lips, demanding entrance.

Dear Reader,

"The hospital mixes up babies" are the words every parent dreads. Garland Warner and Ryker Dugrandpre are no different. In the first book of my new series, The Dugrandpres of Charleston, the deathbed confession of a nurse brings Ryker back into Garland's life. Though the circumstances are less than happy…

Ryker's very reason for living is his daughter, Kai. And Garland loves every minute of her life with her daughter, Amya.

Their worlds are turned upside down after a phone call from the hospital where both children were born. They are stunned when they discover that the little girls they have been raising may not be their biological daughters.

I was inspired to write this story after reading an article about a young couple who lost their lives in a car accident. After their deaths, it was discovered that the baby girl, the lone survivor in the accident, was not their biological daughter. There was a mix-up at the hospital where she was born and her grandparents and the other set of parents involved decided not to switch the babies.

What would you do in this situation? I'd love to hear from you!

Best Regards,

Jacquelin

FOREVER MY BABY

JACQUELIN THOMAS

H HARLEQUIN® KIMANI™ ROMANCE

Recycling programs
for this product may
not exist in your area.

ISBN-13: 978-0-373-86388-4

Forever My Baby

H HARLEQUIN®

Printed in U.S.A.

™ www.Harlequin.com

Jacquelin Thomas has published over fifty-seven books in the romance, women's fiction and young-adult genres. When she is not writing, Jacquelin enjoys spending time with her family, decorating and shopping. Jacquelin can be reached at jacquelinthomas@yahoo.com. She is also on Facebook (www.facebook.com/jacquelinthomas) and Twitter (@jacquelinthomas).

Books by Jacquelin Thomas

Harlequin Kimani Romance

The Pastor's Woman
Teach Me Tonight
Chocolate Goodies
You and I
Case of Desire
Five Star Attraction
Five Star Temptation
Legal Attraction
Five Star Romance
Five Star Seduction
Styles of Seduction
Wrangling Wes
Five Star Desire
Forever My Baby

Visit the Author Profile page
at Harlequin.com for more titles

Chapter 1

"A dying nurse confessed to a possible baby swap just hours before her death. Martha Belle Hayes called for hospital administrators and revealed that she may have mistakenly switched baby girls who were born two years ago on September 8. According to family members, at the beginning of October two years ago, Hayes had abruptly quit her job at the hospital to find work in a clinic.

"Former coworkers say that she'd seemed troubled by something but never confided in anyone. Her mother said Hayes was unwilling to take this secret to her grave and this is why she finally unburdened herself. The state of South Carolina, in cooperation with the hospital, is investigating into how a switch could have taken place."

Ryker DuGrandpre turned off the small, flat-screen television in the kitchen. The story of the baby switch had first broken last night and was the top story on all the news channels. Grateful that it had nothing to do with his family, Ryker glanced over at his two-year-old daughter, his heart filled with love. She sat at the table in a booster seat, patiently waiting for her breakfast.

Kai's presence gave him such joy. She made him feel a bottomless peace and contentment whenever she was around. Despite the tragic circumstances surrounding her birth, his daughter was all that was good in his life.

"Daayee…" she said. "Eat…"

"I hear you. Would you like some applesauce, Kai?"

Her features became more animated as she answered, "Yessh."

"Okay, little lady, but you have to eat your eggs," Ryker said, placing a small plate in front of her.

She glanced down at the plate and then shook her head. "Nooo."

"I thought you like scrambled eggs, princess. You eat them when Jordin makes them."

Scrunching up her nose and pointing to the eggs, Kai responded, "Me no like it."

Ryker chuckled. "Oh, is that your way of saying that you don't like my cooking?"

She grinned at him, her infectious smile echoing through his veins, making his heart sing with delight.

"How about some toast then?" he suggested. "You can't just eat applesauce."

"Yessh."

"I guess I'm going to have to get Jordin to show me how she makes scrambled eggs," he muttered to himself.

Ryker smiled as he heard Kai singing to herself. She loved to sing. He stole a peek at her. Her tiny head was bobbing as she sang softly, and the warm brown spiral curls danced around her cinnamon-tinted face.

He took a piece of toast lathered in apple jelly over to her. "Here you go, sweetie."

"Tank you," Kai murmured.

Ryker planted a kiss on her forehead. "Eat up, Kai."

After they finished breakfast, he cleaned her up and helped her slip on a sundress.

He checked his watch and then said, "It's time to take you to day care. Hurry up and put on your shoes."

Kai rushed off and returned a few minutes later with a pair of pink sandals.

"Don't you want to wear the black ones?"

She shook her head no.

He decided it was better to let her win this round than to risk a tantrum at this point. He had to be in court this morning so he needed to get to his office early.

After dropping Kai off, Ryker drove the short distance to his office. He parked his SUV in his assigned space and hopped out. The May weather was already warming up; the sun was bright and the sky a calming hue of blue. He wanted to be anywhere but inside the law firm founded by his grandparents.

The DuGrandpres had been a solid fixture in Charleston since the 1960s, when his grandparents had relocated from New Orleans with their twin sons and opened the doors of the DuGrandpre Law Offices in the downtown business district.

His uncle, Etienne, and father, Jacques, had taken over the business after their parents retired. Etienne's twin daughters, Jadin and Jordin, were attorneys, as were Ryker and his mother, Rochelle DuGrandpre. Ryker's sister, Aubry, had chosen not to join the family business.

A world-renowned chef in her own right, she owned a restaurant near the Charleston waterfront.

"Jordin, what are you doing here so early?" he asked his twenty-six-year-old cousin as he walked into the office's kitchen. She normally did not come into the office until nine or ten.

"I needed to take care of some paperwork," she responded while surveying the selections of coffees, teas and hot chocolate packets for the Keurig brewer. "Why are you here at this hour?"

"I have court this morning."

"How's my sweet pea?" Jordin asked as she selected a coffee pod and placed it in the machine. "Want one?"

"I'll pass on the coffee, but Kai is great," he said with a smile. "This morning she decided to wear pink sandals with the orange and yellow dress I picked out for her."

Jordin laughed. "It's fine for her to express herself, Ryker. She is her own kind of beautiful. I like that."

"Oh, I need your recipe for making scrambled eggs. Kai doesn't seem to like the way I cook them."

"Cheese," she responded. "Kai likes shredded cheese in her eggs. She won't eat them if they're plain."

"I had no idea." Ryker released a short sigh. "I feel like a terrible father when it comes to things like this. I should know my daughter's likes and dislikes."

"Don't be so hard on yourself." Jordin retrieved her coffee and added sugar. "I only discovered it by accident. I eat mine with cheese and the weekend Kai stayed with me she had some and loved them."

"I was surprised that she wanted scrambled eggs in the first place," he said. "She saw me making some and asked me to share."

"That seems to be her new word," Jordin responded with a chuckle.

Ryker agreed. "I'm always reminding her that she has to share."

Jordin took a sip of her coffee. "She's growing up so fast."

"I'm not ready for it," he uttered. "That little girl is my life. I hate that her mother isn't here to see our daughter." Angela should be there to help him raise Kai. It had never been in the plans for him to be a single father.

Jordin gave his arm a gentle squeeze. "I know that this isn't easy for you, but I want you to know that you're doing a great job, Ryker."

He awarded her with a smile. "Thanks, cousin." They were words he wanted to hear but he wasn't sure he deserved them. He was still a newbie when it came to fathering skills.

"You know I'm here if you ever need me. I love Kai like she's my own."

"That's why I love you," Ryker told her as he checked his watch. "I better get to work. Talk to you later."

The only two ways Ryker had been able to deal with the death of his wife were lavishing all of his attention on his young daughter and staying busy as a managing partner in his family-owned law firm.

He strode with purpose into his corner office, anxious to start his day. It was going to be a long one.

Ryker sat down at his desk, turned on the computer and was soon engrossed in the notes for his upcoming court case. He studied the declarations of the witnesses, committing them to memory.

When he looked up at the wall clock, an hour had

passed. Ryker had about another hour before he had to show up in court, so he relaxed.

Three hours later, he bumped into his other cousin at the courthouse. "What's up, Jadin?"

"Nothing much," she responded with a smile identical to her twin. "I'm waiting to meet with my client. He's not here yet."

"I'm on my way back to the office," Ryker announced. "I'll be glad when this day is over."

"Right now I'll just settle for some lunch," Jadin said. "I didn't have breakfast this morning and I'm starving."

Ryker pulled a Slim Jim out of his attaché case and handed it to Jadin. "Maybe this will tide you over. It works for me."

She embraced him. "Thanks, cousin. See you at some point this afternoon."

When Ryker arrived back at the firm, Jacques Du-Grandpre met him outside his office. "Dad, do you need to see me?" he was inclined to ask.

Tall and solid in stature, his father was a well-respected member of the legal community.

"I just stopped by to see if you wanted to have lunch with me and your mother."

"I'm going to order something from the deli across the street," Ryker responded. "I have a lot of paperwork on my desk and I need to stay on top of it. Why don't we plan something later in the week? Maybe Aubry can join us, too."

Jacques nodded. "That's fine."

Ryker quickly walked into his office and closed the door behind him. He could have taken time to have lunch with his parents, but he was definitely not in the mood to be interrogated by his mother. He already knew the questions she would ask: Have you met anyone special? Don't you think it's time you developed a social life? His mother was on a campaign for him to find a wife so that Kai would have the love of two parents. Rochelle Harper DuGrandpre did not believe that a child could thrive without a mother and a father.

He was determined to prove her wrong. Ryker was not looking for a wife—he was still grieving the loss of Angela, although it would be three years in September since she'd been gone.

Ryker released a sigh of relief when the workday ended at five o'clock. He was looking forward to spending the rest of the evening with Kai. She made life bearable for him. She was truly his reason for living.

Garland Warner laughed in delight as she watched her two-year-old daughter dipping her tiny toes in the surf. They'd been walking hand in hand along the beach, enjoying the cool island breeze swirling around them.

"Mommy…"

"Yes, baby," she prompted.

Pointing, she murmured, "Wadda…"

"Very good, Amya," Garland said with pride. "There's a lot of water out there. It's called the ocean."

"Osen," Amya said, encouraging a grin from Garland.

Garland truly loved her life on Edisto Island. The beaches, saltwater marshes and low-country oaks draped in Spanish moss were a picturesque combination. Historical landmarks were prevalent on the island, providing the backdrop to a rich cultural heritage. The awesome beauty and rich history were why Garland elected to open her high-end children's boutique there.

Garland and Amya usually came to the beach for a stroll before heading home. She found the daily routine a welcome break from the rush of everyday life. And she relished this quality time spent with her daughter.

Garland had desperately wanted to have a child before she turned thirty, so after her last relationship failed she'd decided to take fate into her own hands by using an anonymous sperm donor to get pregnant. Although she'd suffered complications in her pregnancy and during delivery, Garland had delivered a healthy and beautiful little girl.

She glanced down at her daughter and smiled. "C'mon, sweetie. I'm afraid it's time to go home."

Amya did not protest, provoking a soft sigh of relief from Garland. Her daughter loved the ocean as much as she did and often resisted leaving, but this evening was different. Perhaps she was tired, too.

Ten minutes later, they were in the car and on the way home, driving on streets lined with prime beachfront real estate, shops and boutique hotels. Edisto Island was a favorite tourist destination. Garland's shop was only one block over from the main street.

The Fairy Kisses Boutique featured exclusive designer children's dress-up clothes and accessories. Garland had always dreamed of being able to provide kids with outfits for creative, free play all year, along with formal attire for weddings, parties and other affairs. Her store, stocked full of everything from gorgeous and detailed princess and fairy gowns to wizard robes, capes and Native American headdresses, was very popular with the locals and tourists alike.

Garland had grown up in a home where money was tight, but her foster mother had encouraged open, creative play. She had kept a trunk filled with feather boas, hats, dresses, pants and all sorts of accessories to keep her two children occupied.

Having studied psychology and theater in college, Garland believed that pretend play through dressing up enhanced a child's social, emotional, language and thinking skills.

After they got home and had dinner, she gave Amya a bath and dressed her for bed.

"TV," her daughter mumbled, pointing toward the flat screen above the fireplace.

"Just for a little while."

Amya nodded and then turned her attention to the little bear in her arms.

"How is Boo feeling today?" Garland inquired.

"Fine. Her not sick no more."

Whenever Amya was sick, her little bear Boo got sick, too—Amya believed so anyway.

While her daughter watched television, Garland cleaned up the kitchen.

She had to drive to Charleston the next morning for a meeting. For the fourth year in a row, Garland had volunteered to be the chair for a children's festival. Tomorrow they would be discussing potential vendors for the upcoming event.

After getting Amya settled in bed, she strode into her bedroom and walked straight to the closet. She wanted to find the perfect comfortable outfit to wear. Garland pulled out three options, tossed them on the bed and then grabbed two more.

She chuckled at her actions. What did it matter what she wore? It was not as if she were meeting a man. Garland was just going to a meeting and then back to her shop to finish taking inventory.

Garland dropped off Amya at preschool on the island before heading straight to the French Quarter Restaurant located on Bay Street in the historic district of Charleston.

An hour later, she parked her car and climbed out. Horse-drawn carriages and people alike roamed the charming cobblestone streets. The architecture, colorful gardens, historic alleys and courtyards dated back to the colonial era.

She entered the restaurant and walked over to a table near the window, where three people were engaged in conversation. "Good morning," Garland greeted as she pulled out a chair and sat down. "I brought the photographs from the last two festivals. I thought you'd like to see them."

Garland always enjoyed the planning of the annual French Quarter Children's Festival. The other three lunch guests at her table were members of the planning committee, as well.

Two hours later, the meeting concluded. As Garland walked out to her car, she noticed a new children's shop on the next block. *I wonder how long it has been here,* she thought.

Garland walked down to the store and went inside. She navigated slowly through the aisles of clothing for girls and boys. "Quaint," she whispered. *It's a nice store.*

She found a couple of cute dresses for Amya and purchased them.

Her next stop was the bookstore. Garland had not intended to spend this much time in Charleston, but she could never resist an opportunity to buy books.

She walked out twenty minutes later with a bag of books and magazines.

Garland slowed her pace, her eyes widening in surprise as she stared at the man walking toward her in a black suit with faint pinstripes running through the fabric, a classic pale blue shirt and a perfectly knotted black tie.

Ryker DuGrandpre looked as if he'd walked straight out of a magazine. He was a gorgeous, smart but arrogant man who used to tap on her nerves every time she ran into him. He was her brother Parker's best friend and had been his college roommate at the University of South Carolina. Before he had convinced some woman to marry him a few years back, he had had women fall at his feet.

A year behind Parker and Ryker, Garland had managed to withstand the urge to hurl herself at him and had focused on her studies instead. Though it had not been an easy task, considering the huge crush she had had on Ryker.

Then, eight months after graduating from college, her brother had died in a car accident. Ryker had been in law school at the time but had been sure to attend Parker's funeral. That was the last time she had seen him.

He did not seem to know who she was at first, but recognition dawned and he broke into a huge grin. He crossed the distance between them in quick strides.

Ryker embraced her warmly. "Garland, how are you? It's been a long time."

"I'm fine," she responded, his presence giving her joy. "It has been a while. How are you?"

"Life is good. I can't complain."

She smiled. "That's great."

Garland could tell that Ryker was tentative—she knew why and she felt the same way.

"How's your mom doing?" he inquired.

"She's doing the best she can, but I know that she misses Parker. We all do."

"So do I," Ryker confessed. "I wish I had more time to talk to you, but I'm due back in court soon. I was just about to pick up something to eat."

"It's okay," Garland responded. "I need to get back to work, as well. It's good seeing you again." Out of the corner of her eye she could see his eyes tracing her silhouette.

"Here's my card," Ryker said, his lips curling into a delicious smile. "Call me. I'd really like to catch up soon."

For some reason, her body reacted to Ryker. She nodded and reached for his card, but Garland did not intend to make contact with Ryker. Seeing him now brought back the pain of losing her brother. Almost frozen in place, she watched him as he walked in the opposite direction.

She and Parker had been close, despite the fact that his mother and father were her foster parents. Although they initially talked of adopting her, her foster father's untimely death had put an end to that discussion.

Garland had not been disappointed because she knew that she was loved. Her biological mother had died when she was five and her father had been in no condition to raise a child, though she did have a relationship with him, albeit a distant one. He'd remarried when she was ten and his new wife had wanted nothing to do with Garland, leaving her feeling as if she had no real family.

She unlocked her car and got inside. It had been nice seeing Ryker again after all this time. He still possessed those beautiful lips and handsome DuGrandpre features. He was married now, Garland reminded herself. And as far as she was concerned, that ship had sailed. Her one chance with Ryker had come and gone a long time ago.

Chapter 2

When Ryker had first spotted Garland, he'd experienced the weirdest sensation—a strange combination of calm and excitement roiling through his bloodstream like a virus on a mission. The chemistry between them from the first moment Parker had introduced them had blindsided him.

Today, as they had walked toward one another, their gazes locked, Ryker noted a brief reaction of shock and pleasure in her hazel eyes before it faded away into a welcoming stare. Her short haircut was a tumble of soft, light brown curls, tempting him to run his fingers through its silkiness. She was beautiful and still possessed that same youthful glow she'd had in college.

A shred of guilt snaked down his spine because he had not sought out the family after Parker's death. The loss of his best friend had left such an empty hole in his own heart. Then losing his wife shortly after she had given birth to Kai had been almost too much to bear. Kai was all Ryker had left of Angela and he vowed to keep her close always.

He was thankful for his family and the way they'd surrounded him with love and support during each tragedy.

Ryker smiled as he pulled into his parking spot at the law firm and got out of his SUV. He checked his watch as he walked briskly across the lot and into the building.

His mother was in with the office manager. She spotted him and gestured for him to wait for her.

"How is my beautiful granddaughter?" his mother asked as she joined him on the walk to his office.

Rochelle DuGrandpre, hailed as one of the top family law attorneys in the state, was passionate when it came to children. He knew that she often worried about him raising Kai alone.

"She is great," Ryker responded with a smile. "Kai recognizes most of the primary colors and some of her numbers."

"That's wonderful," Rochelle exclaimed. "I'm not surprised, though. She's a DuGrandpre."

Ryker nodded. "That she is."

Rochelle settled down in one of the visitor chairs in front of his desk and studied his face. "Son, how are you doing?"

"I'm fine," he responded in earnest. "I stay busy here at work and when I'm home, my focus is my daughter."

"Why don't you and Kai move in with us?" Rochelle suggested. "It's just your father and me in that huge house. We would love to have you both there."

He shook his head. "Mom, stop worrying about me. I would think you'd be enjoying your empty nest."

"It's nice, but I have always felt that a house comes alive with children."

"Mom, Kai and I are doing fine."

"It's not that I'm worried," Rochelle confessed. "I really miss having young ones at home. With all of you gone, the house seems too quiet."

"Maybe you and Dad should try for a baby," Ryker teased.

"Don't let your father hear you say that," she warned with a chuckle. "He'd have a heart attack."

"You are always talking about how much foster care is needed. Maybe you should consider becoming a foster parent."

Rochelle seemed to consider the idea. "Maybe I'll discuss it with your father, although I already know what he will say."

He laughed. "Dad just wants to enjoy his grandchild. He's not looking to raise more kids."

"Maybe I can change his mind," she said with a smile. "You think?"

He shook his head again. "I seriously doubt it."

Rochelle rose to her feet. "I have a teleconference coming up. Don't forget we're going to the beach this weekend. We're counting on you and Aubry to join us."

"Kai and I will be there," he responded. "She's so excited."

"I can't wait to see my little darling. Maybe I can get her completely potty trained over the weekend. You were out of diapers by the time you turned two years old."

Ryker loved his mother dearly, but there were days

when she frustrated him to no end. She did not seem to know when to let go when it came to him and Aubry.

Although she had never said it, Ryker believed that his mother had little faith in his parenting abilities. It was in the way that she commented on certain things. For example, whenever Kai had an accident, his mother harped on the fact that he should have let *her* conduct the potty training.

Ryker did not want to fail Kai, but his mother often made him feel inadequate as a single parent. He tried not to let her words get to him but failed. The truth was that Angela would have been a great mother. She would have done all the right things and would've known what to do in every situation. But Angela was no longer there. She was gone and he was left to carry on without her.

He'd vowed to be the best father possible to their daughter. Ryker was determined that he would not let Angela down. He had made that promise to her before giving her a final kiss good-bye.

Ryker had never broken any promise he had ever made to Angela. This would be no different.

After two sun-filled days on the beach at Edisto Island, Ryker was ready to return to Charleston. He enjoyed spending time with his family and especially with Kai, but the stacks of cases on his desk awaiting his return Monday morning occupied his mind.

They had just finished having lunch two doors down with his family and were on their way to the car. "Look it…" Kai pointed at the dress in a boutique window. "Pretty."

He glanced up at the name: *Fairy Kisses Boutique.* "I guess you want to go shopping."

Bobbing her head, she responded, "Yessh."

"You are definitely your mother's daughter," he said with a grin. "She loved to shop."

Kai pulled his arm, leading him toward the door.

"I'm coming, honey."

Once inside, Ryker felt like he had been transported to a land filled with fairies and princesses. The atmosphere was magical. Kai, her expression one of pure joy, immediately walked over to a bear on display dressed in a lavender dress with wings.

His gaze landed on a young woman in a navy and white dress with matching flats.

He approached her. "Hey, you…" No matter how subtle her scent was, Ryker was sure he could find her, even in a room filled with a bunch of over-perfumed women.

She turned around to face him. "Ryker…what are you doing here?"

"My little one saw the dresses in the window, so here we are."

Her eyes traveled to his side. "Your daughter is such a cutie."

"Thank you," he responded proudly.

"What brings you to Edisto Island, Ryker DuGrandpre?"

Ryker looked down to see Kai steal another peek at the bear.

"My family and I came here for the weekend," he explained. "We had just had lunch and were heading to the car when Kai discovered this shop." Ryker glanced around. "Are you the manager?"

"I'm the owner, actually."

Ryker did not miss the subtle lifting of her chin as she spoke. "You really have a beautiful store."

She smiled. "Thank you. I'm very proud of it."

"I thought chain stores had taken over, but it's good to see smaller boutiques are still holding strong in the area."

Garland smiled. "This neighborhood happens to be a haven of small and wonderful shops on the island. I love that they are all within walking distance from one another."

She glanced down at Kai again. "She looks like a little fairy princess. I believe I have the perfect outfit for her. It matches the dress that the bear is wearing and comes complete with wings."

"I can already tell that I'm not leaving the store without that bear, so I'll take the outfit, too." Just then, Kai raced from his side and grabbed the bear off the shelf. She quickly returned to his side and tugged at his hand.

The sound of a tinkling bell caught his attention and he heard familiar voices.

"Sorry, Mom, but not this time. I'm really not interested in being hooked up with the nephew of one of your friends."

"And why not?" The woman glanced over at them and said, "We'll discuss this later." She then made her way toward where he, Kai and Garland stood.

"Honey, I thought that I saw you come in here," she said, approaching them.

"My mother," he said by way of introductions.

"Hello. I'm Garland Warner," Garland said cheerfully.

"This is Parker's sister, Mom. She owns this boutique."

"Parker was a wonderful young man. We all miss him." Rochelle's eyes traveled the length of the store. "Your shop is lovely and very original. This is the perfect place for children to explore their fantasies."

"That's exactly what I had in mind when I opened it," Garland said.

Rochelle took Kai by the hand and said to the group, "We're going over here to look at some dresses."

Ryker met Garland's gaze. "I can't believe I've run into you twice in a week after all of these years. It must be fate."

Garland let out a small laugh.

"It really is good to see you again," he told her.

"Ryker, it's nice seeing you, too."

"I still go out to the cemetery to visit Parker."

Garland seemed surprised by his words. "Really?"

He nodded. "He was…is still my best friend."

"I miss him terribly," she admitted. "Losing both Dad and Parker has taken a toll on Mama. She has good days and bad days." After a brief pause, she added, "She's not the same woman you remember, Ryker."

"He took a part of all of us when he left," Ryker stated.

Garland nodded.

"It's good to see that you're doing so well. You have always been such a creative spirit."

"Business is great," she told him. "In fact, I'm thinking of adding a second store in Charleston."

"I think it's a good idea."

Then Garland gave Ryker a sneak peek at a new collection that was not yet on the sales floor. Ryker could feel the heat of his mother's gaze on them as they moved around the store. Her eyes seemed to follow Garland's every movement.

Ryker settled on purchasing several items for Kai, which seemed to thrill Garland.

As she assisted an employee with bagging up his purchases, Ryker peered at her intently.

"Are you sure you don't want to take another look at the Laurent Princess collection in the back?" Garland inquired.

"No, thank you," he said with a grin. "I think that I need to get my daughter out of here right now before she finds something else she wants."

Garland laughed. "I understand. I have to keep my own daughter out of the shop. She thinks she should personally own everything here."

"You have children?" he asked, his eyes straying to her left hand.

"One," she responded. "I have a daughter."

Ryker stepped closer to embrace Garland. "I meant what I said," he told her. "Let's get together soon."

"It was very nice meeting you, Miss Warner," Rochelle interjected. "You have a lovely store."

"Thank you."

"Son, we'd better get Kai home. She's sleepy and you know how she gets when she's tired."

He glanced over at Garland and said, "I hope to hear from you soon."

Ryker gave her one final smile before quickly escorting his daughter out the door. Kai had just spotted another stuffed animal. He needed to get her out of the store before she begged him to buy it.

"Do you know that man?" her employee asked in a low whisper after Ryker and his family had exited the shop.

"He's a DuGrandpre, Robyn," Garland responded with a tiny smile. "Ryker DuGrandpre."

"I knew he looked familiar. There was a huge feature about their law firm in one of the magazines I read recently." Robyn broke into a grin before adding, "He's handsome, don't you think?"

"And very married," Garland stated. "Or didn't you notice the wedding ring on his finger?" However, she noted that he had not mentioned his wife in their conversation at all. But still Ryker *was* very good-looking with firm muscles. It was obvious that he spent a lot of time at the gym working out and taking great care of his body. And his aftershave was as delicious as his appearance.

"I never moved past his face," Robyn responded with a shake of her head.

She laughed. "You're bad."

"There's no harm in looking, Garland."

"Well, I make it a habit to never pay attention to married men."

"When it comes to a married man, I just look at them every now and then," Robyn admitted. "I wouldn't deal with one—that's for sure."

"I know that." Garland knew Robyn well. She had been with her from the inception of the boutique. She was the assistant manager, and Garland loved working with her and having her on the team.

"He may be married, but I couldn't help but notice that he couldn't seem to keep his eyes off you." Robyn straightened a dress that hung lopsided on a hanger.

Garland shrugged in nonchalance. "It's not what you think. He was best friends with my brother. They were college roommates and frat brothers."

"Oh, I had no idea."

"Parker and Ryker had been inseparable," Garland said. "He really took it hard when Parker passed away. I never saw him again after the funeral."

"So this is the first time you two are reconnecting?"

"I actually ran into him in Charleston on Wednesday," she said. "That was almost a week ago."

"So what's up with his mother?" Robyn inquired. "She could barely focus on shopping because she was eyeballing you so hard."

Garland shrugged. "This is the first time I've ever met her. Parker had known her pretty well from spending a lot of time at their house when we were all in college. She was probably making sure I wasn't flirting with her married son."

Garland decided to change the conversation back to work.

"I just ordered the cutest little flower girl dresses," Garland announced. "Wait until you see them, Robyn. The entire collection is stunning."

"I'm glad we're adding more dresses for weddings. They sell very well."

"Go on and say it, Robyn. You were right."

"I was, wasn't I?" she responded with a chuckle. "Garland, I appreciate you so much. You actually listen to your employees."

"So I will be expecting my world's greatest boss mug."

They both laughed.

Garland went to her office a few minutes later to go over sales orders. Her smile broadened over the memory of seeing Ryker again.

But an odd twinge of disappointment interrupted as she reminded herself that he was married with a family.

Chapter 3

"*The State of South Carolina released the results of an investigation into how the switch took place. The report concluded that the cause of the mishap remains a mystery. No evidence was uncovered to suggest foul play and the medical center has heightened its security in order to prevent another inadvertent baby switch...*"

Garland turned off the television as soon as the story of the nurse's deathbed confession came on yet again. It was all everyone had been talking about these past weeks. It made her feel uneasy. But she knew that Amya was her daughter, despite being born on September 8 at that same hospital during the time the nurse was believed to have mistakenly switched the babies.

She sat down on the sofa beside her napping daughter, her thin fingers tensed in her lap. Biting her lip, Garland glanced over at Amya. She refused to believe that the baby switch had anything to do with them. Garland knew without a doubt that Amya was her little girl.

She caught herself glancing uneasily at the blank television screen, her thoughts dark and disquieting. Garland tried to ignore the warning voice in her head. "I'm thinking too much," she whispered. "That story has nothing to do with me. Besides, I would've heard from the hospital by now if this involved Amya."

She inhaled deeply and exhaled slowly.

Garland leaned over and kissed her daughter's forehead. "I love you so much," she whispered.

"Mom…my," Amya murmured sleepily.

She rubbed her back. "Go back to sleep, sweetie."

The doorbell rang.

As she opened the door, she said, "Hey, what are you doing here?" to her best friend, Trina, who stood in the doorway. "I thought you were in Arizona visiting your family. C'mon in here."

"I flew back this morning, so I thought I'd come by to see my bestie and my goddaughter."

"I'm so glad you did," Garland said. "I really missed you and so did Amya. She is napping in the family room. Let's talk in here."

They settled down in the living room.

"Have you heard about the hospital situation?" Trina inquired as she picked up one of the small decorative pillows and held it close to her chest.

Garland nodded. "Can't help but hear about it. It's on the news all of the time."

"Have you been contacted by anyone from the hospital?" Trina asked.

"No," she responded as casually as she could manage. "I don't expect to be contacted because I know that Amya is my child." Biting her lip, Garland looked away.

"Maybe you should have a DNA test completed anyway," Trina suggested. "This way there will never be any doubt in your mind."

Garland awkwardly cleared her throat. "I don't have any doubt, Trina."

Trina eyed her in bewilderment. "How could you not? Any parent who gave birth to a daughter on that day should be worried."

Garland stirred uneasily in her chair. "They're sure it was a girl?"

Trina nodded. "Yeah. There were six girls born that day within a four-hour period."

"I feel sorry for those parents," Garland said. "I really do, but I don't need a DNA test to tell me what I already know. I have the child I gave birth to—she is a part of me."

"For the record, I believe Amya is yours, as well."

"Then let's change the subject, please."

"Sure," Trina responded hesitantly.

Garland silently struggled with the uncertainty that had been aroused by their conversation.

"While I was in Arizona, I reconnected with an old boyfriend."

"Really? How did that go?"

Trina broke into a grin. "It actually went very well."

Garland smiled. "Is this the one from college you were telling me about?"

Her friend nodded. "Yeah. He works for a pharmaceutical company, but get this…he's been thinking about relocating to Charleston. He has a frat brother in the area who's offered him a nice position."

"Wow…that's wonderful."

"He did mention the guy is single, Garland."

She quickly shook her head. "I have no time for men right now. I want to focus on Amya and my shop."

"Garland, I know that you've been through a lot, but you can't lock your heart away forever."

"I'm not," she responded. "I just don't have any more time for lies and games. Maybe in a few years I'll consider dating again, but right now Amya needs me most."

"What do you need, Garland?" Trina inquired. "You can't live your life just for your daughter or your business."

"I'm human, Trina," she uttered. "Of course, I would like to spend time with someone special. But right now that's something I can live without. Besides, I have extremely bad taste in men. Remember Noah?"

Trina burst into laughter. "I do."

"He was supposed to steal my heart, not my flat-screen TV and my laptop."

"Noah had a serious drug addiction."

"I had no idea, though."

"Well, he did apologize to you," Trina stated. "That's more than you got from Calvin."

"I had no expectations of Calvin being sorry for anything. He was a dog and he expected me to be okay with it."

"He was a screwup for sure." Trina shook her head. "Hey, I've had my share of nightmare relationships, as well."

"Our lives have been filled with so much more glamour and romance since we got rid of those deadbeat dates," Garland said with a chuckle.

"So far, this guy I'm seeing again is good," Trina stated. "He's still on my mandatory trial period, though."

Garland shook her head at her friend's usual antics. "When am I going to meet Mr. Wonderful?"

"I said he was good. He's not wonderful yet—if he survives probation, then he might graduate to wonderful."

Garland laughed. "He might as well be dating someone of the highest social class in society the way you're vetting him."

"Honey, he is dating royalty," Trina interjected. "I am a queen."

"I hear you," Garland said.

"Enough about me. Now I'm serious—it's time for you to get back into the dating pool. Amya can't be your whole life, sweetie."

"For now, she's enough," Garland insisted. "Speaking of your godchild, it's time we woke her up."

"Thanks for taking care of Kai for me," Ryker told Jordin when he arrived home shortly after 6 p.m. "Her teacher was sick and I didn't want to expose Kai to whatever may be going around. The administrator said it is some type of stomach virus."

"It's my pleasure. You know how much I love that little girl." She rose to her feet and began putting away a stack of papers.

He gestured toward her laptop. "Were you able to get any work done?"

Jordin nodded. "Quite a bit, actually. Kai watched television and played with her toys until lunch. After we ate, I took her to the park. She took a nap as soon as we got back."

Her eyes traveled to the television in the family room. A news reporter was going over the dead nurse's confession.

"Can you believe that?" Jordin asked. "I just don't understand why that nurse didn't come forward sooner, especially if she even suspected she may have switched the babies. This could have been corrected much sooner. It must have haunted her all this time, from what I'm hearing."

"I suppose she was worried more about her job," Ryker responded. "It was selfish for her to keep this secret. She's not even sure she gave the babies to the wrong parents. It may create upset for no reason at all."

"This is true, Ryker, but we have no idea what her life was like," Jordin pointed out. "Maybe all she had was her work as a nurse. At least she left the hospital and found other work so that she couldn't make the same mistake again."

He shrugged in nonchalance. "It was still wrong."

She nodded. "You're right. I just feel bad for her."

Jordin followed Ryker into his office. "Kai was born at that very same hospital on the same day," she said. "Yet you don't seem worried about this at all."

He met her gaze. "I'm not worried, Jordin. I know that she is my daughter. I'm sure I would know if she wasn't my child."

"Would you really?" She sat down in the plush leather chair across from Ryker.

"What are you trying to say?"

"We all love her, Ryker, but wouldn't you want to know if there's a chance that you were given the wrong baby? It would mean that your biological child is still out there in the world somewhere." Jordin studied his face. "You mean, with everything that's going on, you haven't considered this possibility at all?"

"No, I haven't. Kai is my daughter, Jordin," Ryker stated in a tone that brooked no argument. "I feel bad for the people involved. If it happened to me, I would sue the hospital for everything it's worth and I hope they will, too. In fact, I may offer my services pro bono to the parents. This is something awful to have to deal with. I don't know what I'd do if someone came to me saying that Kai may not be my child."

Jordin's expression was solemn. "I don't know what we'd do either, quite honestly. But I know we'd find a way if that were ever the case. We're a strong family. Ryker, we'd figure it out."

Jordin then collected her belongings before moving toward the door. "Remember, anytime you need me, I'm a phone call away."

Ryker offered her a slight smile and watched from the doorway as she walked to her car, which was parked directly out front.

After Jordin pulled off, Ryker walked back inside, secured the door, and spent time with his daughter until it was time for her to go to bed.

Kai now settled and sleeping, Ryker sat down in the family room to watch television. During a commercial, Ryker checked his voice mail messages. Only one in particular caught and held his attention—the one from the hospital.

Why are they calling me? he wondered. It was probably just to assure him that his daughter was not affected by the current uproar. With that in mind, Ryker did not dwell on the message. He made a mental note to call the chief of staff tomorrow, then filed it away for the rest of the night.

The next day, Ryker scanned through the stack of messages his secretary had handed him when he arrived in the office. His gaze paused on one note in particular—a second message from the hospital. He immediately asked his secretary to hold his calls, then he walked back to his office. He had no idea how long he sat there, trying to figure out what all this could mean. Ryker was so focused on that one note that he did not notice his father's arrival.

"Son…"

He looked up to find his father standing in the doorway. "Is everything okay? You look like you've received some troubling news."

"I have a message from the chief administrator at the hospital." Ryker ripped out the words in annoyance. "They left one at the house, too."

"What is this about?" Jacques inquired. "Does this have anything to do with my granddaughter?"

"I don't know," he responded, sounding curt. "But I assure you, Kai is my daughter. There were other girls born on that day. This has nothing to do with us."

Jacques nodded. "I suppose they could be contacting everyone born on that day."

"That's what I figured," he said. "I don't like them involving my daughter in this mess-up."

"Go talk to them, son. This way we can get everything straight."

Ryker clenched his mouth tighter, his vexation evident. "I'll give the chief hospital administrator a call. Maybe we can settle this over the phone."

Jacques shook his head. "I think you should meet with them face-to-face."

Ryker mulled it over before responding. "You might be right. I'm going to set up an appointment with the chief to find out why he's been trying to reach me. The sooner I get this over with, the better."

Chapter 4

Garland hung up the telephone and then turned to Robyn. "I need to take a quick break. I'll be in my office if you need me."

Once Garland sat down at her desk, she picked up the phone with trembling hands and dialed. "Trina, I just got off the phone with someone from the hospital," Garland said as soon as her friend answered. "I have to meet with the chief of staff in a couple of hours."

"Are you okay?"

"I don't know what this is about, Trina. Amya is my daughter." Her daughter was her whole world. Not that unknown child somewhere, the one who might look like her, but this child—the one she'd nursed and diapered, whose toes she'd tickled and counted, the one who squeezed her hand.

"Do you want me to go with you?"

"No, I'll be fine," Garland focused passionately on only one thought: Amya was hers. "It may turn out to be nothing."

"Maybe they just want to reassure you that everything has been straightened out."

"I hope so," she replied."

"Why don't you let me go with you, Garland?" Trina offered again. "I'm sure this is nerve-racking. It certainly would be for me."

"Maybe it might be a good idea to have you accompany me. I'm so nervous right now that I'm not sure I can even drive."

"You don't have to worry about driving, Garland. I'll pick you up."

"Okay," she stated. "Thanks, Trina."

Garland was grateful for her friend. This was not something she wanted to go through alone. She tried to keep a positive outlook. Perhaps the hospital was just being thorough. Maybe they wanted to reassure her that Amya was truly her daughter. Garland did not want to consider any other option. The thought made Garland sick to her stomach.

She checked her watch as she headed back to the sales floor. She said to Robyn, "I need to run out for a couple hours."

Trina arrived ten minutes later.

When they pulled into the hospital parking lot in Charleston, Garland felt the onset of fear and the prickle of goose bumps on her skin. "Trina, I'm not sure I can do this."

"You can," her friend assured her. "I'll be right beside you."

She smiled at Trina. "I'm so glad that you insisted on coming with me. I don't know what I'd do if you weren't here."

Suddenly, Garland froze as her eyes met Ryker's when she walked into the waiting area of the hospital chief's office. "What is he doing here?" she whispered.

Trina followed her gaze. "Who is he?"

"Ryker DuGrandpre," Garland responded, her voice full of dread. "Lord, I hope this isn't about his little girl, too. She's about Amya's age."

"Do you know him?"

She nodded. "He and my brother were best friends. He came to my store not too long ago with his daughter. Talk about the most adorable little girl." As they approached Ryker, Garland noted how his dark eyes gave off a tortured dullness of disbelief.

When he switched all that intensity to her, she hesitated, half in anticipation, half in trepidation.

"Ryker…" Garland began. "Please tell me that you're not here about the baby switching."

Before he could respond, Trina offered him her hand and quickly interjected. "I'm Trina Mason. Garland is a close friend of mine."

Ryker offered a polite smile. "I'm afraid I am, Garland," he said. "And it's nice to meet you, Miss Mason."

Garland struggled to hold her composure. This surely could not be happening.

His eyebrows rose a fraction. "Your daughter was also born September eighth?"

"Yes." Mixed feelings surged through her and Garland fought to control them.

They stared at each other across a sudden silence.

This was any parent's worst nightmare and now she

was forced to contend with a DuGrandpre, the very influential, wealthy elite of Charleston society.

As they entered the hospital chief's office, her eyes swept the area, looking for Ryker's wife. Surely, she would be there with him. Garland was curious about the woman he chose as a mate for life. A thread of jealousy snaked down her spine, but she quickly dismissed it.

"Why don't you have a seat?" Trina suggested, giving Garland a slight tug on the arm. "I'll let them know you both are here."

She nodded. "I think I will." Garland feared she would pass out if she did not sit down right away.

Rigid, she sat in a nearby chair, fingers tensed in her lap and her eyes searching.

"Who are you looking for?" Trina asked in a whisper when she returned from the receptionist's desk.

"His wife," Garland responded. "Don't you think it's odd that she's not here with him?"

"Maybe she is meeting him here or she didn't want to come," Trina replied, shrugging in nonchalance.

"I wouldn't be anywhere else in this situation," she muttered.

Ryker was watching her from his nearby seat. Garland became increasingly uneasy under his scrutiny. She cleared her throat noisily. Her eyes then landed on him. She looked away hastily and then moved restlessly in her chair.

"I hate all this waiting."

As soon as the words left her mouth, a young woman came out to get both her and Ryker.

"I'll be right out here," Trina promised.

Garland nodded. "Thanks," she whispered as she rose to her feet.

Ryker waited for her near the door.

Inside the office, they sat side by side.

Two of the people in attendance were lawyers—they had that look about them, Garland decided. The other was the chief of staff.

The conversation began with a host of apologies to both her and Ryker.

"Why are we here?" Ryker asked, getting straight to the point.

Dr. Walter Rainey, the chief of staff, looked like a cornered animal. He straightened his tie for the fourth time since they had entered in his office. "As you may know, certain information has come to light that two baby girls born in this hospital on September eighth may have been switched."

"We are well aware of this situation," Ryker stated. "I'll ask again. What is it that you want from us?"

"We are asking that parents agree to DNA testing to determine whether this was, indeed, what happened."

"Dr. Rainey, what I'd like to know is how the hospital staff is really so incompetent as to make a mistake like this? I was under the impression that babies were tagged with a wristband immediately after birth."

Garland gripped the edge of her chair as panic whipped around the perimeter of her anger. How could they screw up like this? Didn't they understand the preventable angst caused in this unfortunate situation?

Before Dr. Rainey could respond, Ryker added, "What about the other baby girls born that day?"

"They have all been tested and match," Dr. Rainey interjected. "Miss Warner's daughter was born within ten minutes of your daughter's birth."

"Have you considered that the nurse simply assumed

that she made a mistake?" Ryker inquired. "When my wife had the heart attack, I know things got a bit hectic, so maybe the nurse isn't really sure what happened that day."

Garland glanced at Ryker, noting his pained expression. His wife had had a heart attack during her delivery. From the look on his face, she could only assume that she had not survived. She wanted to reach over and offer him comfort but decided it was not what he needed now.

"Yes, we have considered this and it is the outcome that we hope for," the chief of staff stated. "However, in order to be sure, we would like to test your daughters."

"I'm not interested in having a DNA test done," Garland blurted out, her emotions out of control. "Amya is my biological daughter and I know it."

"Miss Warner, I'm very sorry for having to put you and Mr. DuGrandpre through this, but the only way that we can clear this up is through DNA," Dr. Rainey explained. "We are only following up on the possibility that the babies were in fact switched."

"He's right," Ryker stated. "We need to know for sure."

"You have doubts?" she asked.

"No, I don't," he responded. "Kai is my daughter and I'm absolutely sure of it. I just want this over and done with."

"I can't believe this is happening…" Garland muttered. "My baby was with me the entire time I was in the hospital."

"According to the notes, there was a point when she was taken to the nursery," Rainey said.

Garland thought about his words. "The nurse took her out of the room shortly after she was born, but it was only for a little while." She glanced over at Ryker. "It wasn't that long."

"I know how unsettling this is, Garland, but as soon as we get the results of the DNA tests, our lives can return to normal," Ryker told her.

She gave a slight nod. "This is crazy. I know that my daughter is my child. I'm surprised that you don't feel the same way."

"Regardless of how I feel, we need to know the truth."

After the appointments were set for the DNA testing, Garland and Ryker walked out of the office together.

"Ryker, I had no idea about your wife," she said. "I'm sorry."

"It happened so quickly," he said. "She never even got to see our daughter. At least she was spared this situation."

Trina walked over to them in haste. "You okay?" she asked Garland.

"They want to do DNA tests on our daughters."

"Are they saying that they were switched?"

"The hospital is hoping to prove that they were not," Ryker stated. "I suppose they hope to avoid any lawsuits over this situation."

"I don't think there will be any lawsuits coming from us," Garland said. "We have the right children."

Ryker agreed. "After the tests, we all can put this behind us."

"It's nice seeing you again, although I wish it were on better terms," she told him.

"After this is over, we'll go out for drinks and laugh about this."

Garland smiled. "Absolutely."

Ryker nodded and walked off in the opposite direction.

Once inside the car, Garland said, "I remember seeing a photo in the newspaper of a little boy screaming and reaching for the only parents he'd ever known while the biological father carried him away. Only now when I think about that picture, I see Amya being ripped out of my arms."

"That's not going to happen," Trina assured her. "You know Ryker DuGrandpre. Do you think he'd do something like that to you? Parker's little sister?"

Garland began to shake. She could hear herself gasping and panting for air.

Trina reached over and took her hand. "Relax, sweetie. Slow down your breathing."

Tears rolled down her cheeks. "I can't deal with this," Garland whispered. "What if I'm wrong about Amya? What if it turns out that she's Ryker's daughter?"

"Then it would mean that he has been raising your little girl," Trina reminded her.

"Why did that nurse have to stir up this trouble? We were all fine before this."

In her shop the next day, Garland decided that she must be in shock. She felt strange, cold and frightened.

That feeling stayed with her even as she picked up Amya from preschool. Garland relished having her daughter in her arms.

Later in the evening, Garland crept down the hall to Amya's bedroom and hovered over her daughter's tiny frame. Under a pink and white lace comforter, Amya slept peacefully. She could just make out her face in the glow from the nightlight.

Garland closed her eyes on a soft agonized exhalation.

* * *

Ryker stole a peek at the clock and muttered a curse. He had left the office later than he'd planned and if traffic did not pick up, he was going to be late picking up Kai. He closed his eyes for a moment. If only he knew what he was doing. If only Angela were alive to help him raise their daughter.

He did not like to ask his mother for help. It provided her with the opportunity to point out all of the reasons he should move back home.

Five minutes later Ryker pulled up in front of the Cobblestone Day School, considered the best school and day care in Charleston. Angela had chosen it when she was pregnant. They had toured the school together.

"Isn't this perfect?" she had asked him, her eyes sparkling with pleasure.

In that moment, Ryker glimpsed a vision of the little girl who had become the center of his life—the little girl with the same joy as her mommy. She was happy and filled with giggles. Pain stabbed at him, prompting Ryker to rub his chest. He had never once considered any other day care for Kai. He had vowed to raise their daughter as Angela would have wanted.

Ryker rushed into the building and walked briskly to his daughter's classroom. As soon as he entered, Kai erupted to her feet and into his arms.

"Dayee."

"I'm here, baby. Daddy's here."

"Wanna go home," she mumbled against his shoulder.

He kissed her cheek. "We're going home right now."

Ryker spoke with her teacher, inquiring about Kai's day. "I see she had an accident," he said, noticing that she was not wearing the same outfit he had dressed her in that morning.

"She did, but she's doing much better about letting us know when she needs to potty. This happened when she was on the playground. She was playing and waited too late."

"Wanna go home," Kai repeated.

Her teacher patted her gently on the back. "I'll see you tomorrow, Kai."

"Morrow."

They settled into his car, and Ryker was grateful for the distraction of merging traffic. The weather had been clear upon his arrival to the school, but it was now misting rain.

Minutes later, there was a steady drizzle and the swishing sound of the windshield wipers filled the vehicle.

Ryker thought back on his relief that Kai no longer held on to him and screamed when he dropped her off in the mornings. He had felt like the worst parent in the world when her teacher had to pry his daughter's fingers off him.

That vision haunted him now. Would Garland do the same thing—pry Kai's fingers and haul her away, leaving him with the image of his daughter's tear-streaked face, her eyes desperate and pleading, leaving him only with a memory that would haunt him for the rest of his days?

He could not let that happen. He would *not* let it happen, Ryker vowed.

Ryker drove straight into the garage. Kai did not stir when he turned off the engine and opened the door to get out. She had fallen asleep during the short ride home, apparently worn out by her eight-hour day at the school. Stomach knotted with tension, he bolted out of the car and rounded the SUV to get his daughter out of her car seat.

He carried his sleepy daughter into the house and placed her on the sofa. Ryker tickled her to try waking her up.

"Top it," Kai moaned.

A look of tenderness leaped into his eyes and his chest clenched tight around his heart as he looked at her.

Outside, the skies opened up and began to release a load of rain. Ryker was grateful to have made it home before the storm.

He attempted once more to wake Kai up.

"Nooo," she complained.

"Honey, don't you want to eat dinner?"

Kai rewarded him with a nod.

"How about spaghetti?" Ryker suggested.

"Ghetti," she whispered.

He picked her up and carried her to the bathroom to wash her face. "Let's get you freshened up for dinner."

Kai looked up at him and smiled. "Dayee…"

He planted a kiss on her forehead.

Ryker recalled the day Kai was born. The truth was that he had not even looked at her after she was delivered via emergency C-section. He had been holding Angela's hand, pleading with her not to leave him, willing her to live.

It had soon become evident that she needed to be hooked up to machines to sustain her life. Ryker had refused to leave her side. Angela had lain there in the hospital bed for two days, her beautiful eyes closed, breasts rising and falling with the hissing of the respirator. When doctors had offered no hope of her recovery, Ryker and his in-laws had agreed that she should be taken off the machines.

Kai had been a day old when he'd finally held her in his arms. He'd brought her in to meet her mother, although Angela had been unaware. They had decided on a name long before she had been born, so Ryker had honored his late wife's request.

He recalled that the infant had showed no resemblance to her mother, much to his relief and disappointment. There were days when it was a blessing that he did not see his beloved Angela every time he looked at Kai. Then it hit Ryker—Garland's little girl might possess Angela's bright smile and big personality. He then released a low groan.

But nobody was going to take Kai from him. Not even Garland. Parker had entrusted him to look after his sister before he took his last breath, but Ryker was not going to let her take his daughter from him.

Ryker had no idea how long he'd been sitting in his car watching Garland. She was outside her shop talking to a customer. He could hardly take his eyes off her, especially the warm sienna color of her hair.

A chill snaked down his spine.

It was the same color as Kai's curly tresses. The first time he and Garland had met, her hair had been shoulder-length and she'd worn it in its natural wavy state. Now, she wore it short in a pixie-style cut.

His late wife's hair had been dark brown, whereas his own was black. It seemed strange, but he had never given much thought to the color of his daughter's hair before now. Ryker shook off his suspicions. All this talk about a baby switch was beginning to get to him.

He got out of the car when it looked like Garland's conversation was winding down.

She seemed surprised to see him. "Ryker?"

"I'm not stalking you, I promise."

Garland gave him a tiny smile. "It's always good to see you."

"Then why do I get the feeling that you'd like to be anywhere else than right here with me?"

"I can't believe that this is happening," she murmured. "But once we get the test results back—I truly hope that this nightmare will be over."

"Either way this turns out, I want you to know that you have nothing to fear from me, Garland."

"I'm glad to hear it." She raised her eyes, meeting his gaze. "I'm sure you didn't come all the way here just to tell me that. Why are you really here, Ryker?"

"Do you have a picture of your daughter?"

Her expression appeared guarded. "Yes, I do. Why?"

"I'd like to see it," Ryker said, ignoring the pensive shimmer in the shadow of her eyes.

"I'm not sure that's a good idea," she responded. "Right now, we shouldn't even consider the idea that our girls were switched." Garland reached for the door handle. "I have to get back to my shop, but I want to know something…"

"What is it?"

"How are you coping with all of this? I'm frustrated because I know that Amya is the little girl I gave birth to and held in my arms."

"This isn't easy for me, either, but we have to find out the truth."

"Ryker, I already *know* the truth," Garland responded with a subtle lifting of her chin.

"We still need to talk."

She shook her head. "Not right now. It can wait until after the results come back. We can celebrate then."

"I had that same belief until a short while ago." Ryker held out a photo of his daughter. "Look at her hair."

Garland's lips quivered. "Don't do this."

"As much as I want to believe otherwise, we have to consider that our daughters may…" His voice trailed off. He couldn't bring himself to finish the sentence. "Your daughter has dark hair, right?"

"Amya's hair is almost black," she admitted, "but it doesn't mean anything."

"True, but Kai's hair is the same color as yours. Trust me, Garland—this is not the kind of confusion I want for myself or Kai."

"Then you need to stop seeing something that isn't there, Ryker. Your daughter could have inherited her hair color from someone in her ancestral line on either you or her mother's side. You know that."

"You're right," he admitted. "I'm letting this whole thing make me crazy."

"You can't do that, Ryker."

"I hope that I didn't scare you by coming here like this," Ryker stated. "I wanted to talk to you about the girls just in case…"

Garland shook her head. "We don't need to deal with this unless there is a reason for it. Let's just wait for the DNA results."

Ryker nodded. "I guess you're right. I don't need to go looking for trouble."

"I was just about to grab something to eat," she said. "Why don't you join me?"

"Sure."

They walked side by side over to the restaurant across the street from the boutique. The hostess grabbed two menus and led them to a table by the window.

"I can't believe you're all grown up," Ryker told her as they settled in their seats.

Garland chuckled. "I'm only a year younger than you."

"I wish Parker could see you now. He would be so proud of you." Ryker picked up his menu but did not look at it. "He was always bragging about how smart you were."

"He was going to be a great lawyer," she murmured. "Parker planned to work in your family's law firm, you know."

Ryker nodded. "We talked about it all of the time. We took our LSATs together. Parker called me when he got his acceptance to law school. His letter came a week before mine. I was worried that I wouldn't get in."

"I was happy for you both," she responded.

But that happiness was short-lived, Ryker added silently. A few months later, Parker was dead. He had come home to visit the family and had gone out with friends that night. The visit had turned tragic when a drunken driver had crashed into his car, killing him.

Ryker was supposed to have come home with him, but he'd changed his mind at the last moment.

"What are you thinking about?" Garland inquired.

"Your brother," he responded. "I always wonder if things would've turned out different if I'd come home with him that weekend."

"Maybe not," she responded. "Instead of losing only

Parker, we might have lost you, too. God chose to take my brother at a good time. He was a devout Christian. I miss him terribly, but I find peace in that he will forever be with the Lord."

"You're right about that. He used to drive me crazy with all of his Bible studying, but he found so much harmony in it."

When the waitress approached the table, Ryker placed his order after Garland.

"So when did you get married?" Ryker asked. "I have to tell you that I feel some type of way over not receiving a wedding invitation."

"You didn't get one because I never got married," Garland stated.

"Oh."

She laughed. "You don't have to sound like that, Ryker. I'm okay with being single."

"Are you and your daughter's father in contact with one another?"

Garland shook her head. "I am both mother and father to her."

Their food arrived, but Garland didn't seem to have an appetite once her plate was placed in front of her.

"Could you bring me a to-go box, please?" she requested before the waiter left the table.

"You aren't hungry?" Ryker inquired.

"Not really."

"I feel the same way," he confessed.

After both filled their to-go boxes with their uneaten lunch Ryker walked Garland back to her shop.

Before heading back home after she left the shop, Garland decided to pay her mother a visit. It was time to let her in on what was going on with Amya and Ryker.

She let herself into the house where she'd spent most of her childhood. "Mama, it's just me," Garland called out.

"I'm in the family room."

Garland followed the direction of her mother's voice. "How are you feeling?"

Elaine Moscot was lying on the couch in a pair of silk pajamas and watching television. She sat up when she entered the room. "I'm okay, outside of a few body aches and pains."

"Is there anything I can do for you to make you feel better?" Garland asked.

Her mother shook her head. "I don't want you worrying about me. I'm going to be fine, darling. I just need to get some rest."

"I hope you're not overdoing it when you volunteer at the schools."

"I enjoy working with the kids, Garland. My depression has really been trying to take over, but I'm not going to let it keep me from living." Elaine surveyed her daughter's face. "Honey, what's going on with you? I can tell something's bothering you."

"Mama, have you been paying attention to the story about the baby switch at Charleston Memorial Hospital?"

"I've heard something about it. Why?"

"Amya may not be the little girl I gave birth to, Mama. The hospital wants to have all of the girls born on September eighth tested through DNA. All of the other girls have been tested except for Amya and a little girl named Kai."

"What?"

"Her mother died during delivery, so there was a lot going on. And you know about my complications …

Anyway, the nurse on duty that day recently said on her deathbed that she may have unintentionally switched the babies."

"Where is this other baby...the one that may be our baby girl? Is she still in the area?"

"She's in Charleston with Ryker DuGrandpre," Garland announced. "His daughter, Kai, may be my daughter, Mama."

"Ryker?"

Garland nodded. "I had no idea his wife was pregnant or that they were at the hospital the same time I was there. I never even saw them."

"They were probably in that section where the VIPs give birth," her mother said. "I never saw him, either." She paused a moment before asking, "What are you going to do?"

"We can't do anything but wait on the results of the DNA tests," Garland explained. "After that, if the girls really were switched, then Ryker and I have to find a way to deal with this. Whatever we decide, we just have to make sure the girls' happiness and security come first."

"Ryker of all people... This is something," her mother murmured almost to herself. "I know she was well taken care of—our little girl."

"We don't know anything yet, Mama. Regardless, I love Amya and she will always be my little girl."

"Well, of course, hon. I understand that."

"Mama, I want Amya to be mine. I don't want to lose my little girl." Her misery was like a steel weight around her.

Chapter 5

Garland picked up the telephone to call Trina. "I had lunch with Ryker earlier and he thinks that Amya may be his biological daughter."

"Why?" Trina asked. "Why would he think that?"

"Ryker showed me a photograph of his daughter. He pointed out that her hair is the same color as mine. He asked if Amya had dark hair. I told him yes but that her father had dark hair, as well."

"You don't know that for sure."

"I wasn't going to tell him that. I'm not giving Ryker DuGrandpre anything to use against me."

"Aren't you curious, too, Garland?" Trina inquired. "Don't you want to know if Amya is yours for sure?"

"I do and I don't," she confessed. "I guess what worries me most is if she is not my baby, it's not like I can easily dismiss the life I shared with her. I raised her and she belongs to me. She's mine."

"And if Kai is also yours? What then?"

"I don't know, Trina," Garland answered with frustration. "I have no idea." She bit her lip until it throbbed like her pulse.

Once home, Garland kept Amya close to her throughout the evening.

This was her little girl—she had to be. If things turned out otherwise, she would fight Ryker with everything she had to keep her daughter. If Kai turned out to be hers… Garland knew that she would be unable to turn her back on her, either. She also knew that Ryker would never give up his child easily.

The image of the little boy torn away from his family floated to the forefront of her mind again. Although she had been told by a psychologist that the girls were young enough to be switched back and be okay, Garland was not willing to risk it. She could not put Amya or Kai through such emotional turmoil. In time, they might not remember, but Garland was not sure she could live with the memory or the heartache.

Despite what the DNA tests would prove, Ryker doubted he could give up Kai because he loved her dearly. He knew that Garland had to feel the same way about Amya. Switching the children back would be completely out of the question as far as he was concerned. But he also could not walk away from his natural child…

He released a groan when he heard his doorbell ring. Ryker knew it could only be his mother. As he opened the front door, he said, "Hey, Mom."

She brushed past him into the house. "If you'd given me a call, I would've met you at the hospital."

"Mom, I didn't call you because I didn't need you there."

Rochelle turned to face him, her expression one of hurt. "I only meant as a source of support."

He met her gaze. "I didn't mean to hurt you, but I don't need you to fight my battles."

"It's just that you've been through so much, son."

"I'm fine," Ryker insisted with returning impatience.

"I came to see my grandbaby," Rochelle announced. "I hope it's okay that I'm here."

"She's watching television in her room. I was just about to check on her." He knew that the real reason for his mother's visit was to see if things were running smoothly in his home.

He followed her to his daughter's room and stood in the doorway.

"Ganma," Kai exclaimed with joy as soon as Rochelle entered the bedroom. "Ganma…look," she said, pointing to the TV screen.

"Is that Mickey Mouse?" Rochelle asked.

"Nicky Nouse," Kai repeated with a nod.

She pulled the little girl into her arms. "I love you so much."

"TV," Kai fussed.

"I'm sorry," Rochelle said. "I didn't mean to take you away from your movie."

Ryker chuckled. "She loves her Mickey Mouse."

They walked down to the family room.

"I suppose it's time we plan a trip to Disney World then." Rochelle sat down on the sofa and laid her purse on the coffee table. "We could do it in the fall when it's not so hot."

"I'll think about it," he responded. *She is still trying to be in control,* Ryker thought.

Ryker met his mother's gaze. "You haven't weighed in on this baby-switching issue at the hospital. I know that you want to talk about it."

"Son, you know how much we love Kai," Rochelle stated in a low voice. "If it turns out that she is not your biological daughter, what are you going to do?"

"I honestly don't know, Mom," he responded. "She is my whole life. I want my biological child, but letting Kai go..." He could not finish his sentence.

"Perhaps there's a way that we can keep them both," his mother suggested.

"Mom, how can you say that? You don't think Garland will want her child?" Ryker asked, hoping for a plausible explanation.

"She's a single mother," Rochelle announced.

"How do you know that?" he questioned, although he already knew the answer.

"I did some checking on Miss Garland Warner," she told him. "I would think she would desire the best for her daughter, and we can give her that. She would have liberal visitation, of course."

"I know that you mean well, but you're getting ahead of yourself, Mom. Let's just wait for the DNA results to come in. I'm sure they will only confirm what I already know—that Kai is my daughter." He decided not to let his mother in on his suspicions. There was still a chance that Kai was his biological daughter. "Besides, I'm not going to do anything that would hurt Garland."

"We have to be prepared in the event that Kai is not our blood," Rochelle argued, cutting into his thoughts. "Having a plan of action is important. As for Garland,

I know you feel some loyalty to her because of Parker, but I'm sure he would want what's best for the children, as well."

Ryker knew his mother believed it would be best to raise the girls together in a stable, two-parent home. One of his mother's greatest frustrations was witnessing how some parents mistreated their children by being abusive or neglectful. Rochelle believed and had often told him that cruelty to children was the cause of most societal problems.

"Mom, I don't want to dwell on this right now," he stated firmly. Ryker looked away hastily and then moved restlessly in his chair.

Rochelle's phone began to ring.

Ryker broke into a grin. "That's Dad calling—it's time for you to go home."

She smiled. "He's such a good man, your father, but he wouldn't eat if I didn't provide dinner."

"You've spoiled him," Ryker told her. "This is your fault."

Rochelle dug into her purse and pulled out her cell phone. "I'm calling your sister and ordering takeout. I'm not in the mood to cook tonight."

Ryker walked his mother out of his house to her car. "I'll see you tomorrow in the office."

She kissed his cheek. "I love you, son."

"I love you, too."

He closed the door and walked back to the living room. As he settled on the couch, Garland entered into Ryker's thoughts, bringing to mind one night in particular.

He had run into her when she was leaving the library. Ryker was heading back to his dorm room when he spotted Garland.

"What are you doing out here so late?" he asked her.

"I needed to do some research for a report. What are you up to?"

"I'm about to make sure you get to your dorm safely," Ryker said with a grin. *"Parker would never forgive me if I let anything happen to you."*

"You don't have to do this," Garland said. *"I can make it from here."*

He shook his head. "I'm not going to leave you alone."

"Then you're going to have to walk me to Pizza Hut because I'm hungry."

"Sounds good to me."

Fifteen minutes later, they were seated at a booth near the window, talking and laughing while waiting on their pepperoni and bacon pizza to arrive.

It was the first time Ryker had spent one-on-one time with Garland. It was also when he'd acknowledged his attraction to her.

"I really like you, Garland, but I know that Parker would have a problem with me seeing his little sister."

"Parker is my brother. He doesn't tell me what to do or who I can see, Ryker. He may not like it at first, but he'll get over it."

"You are really someone special, Garland."

"You make me feel special," she responded. *"You make me feel as if there's nothing I can't do. I really appreciate that."*

Garland had invited him up to her room. Her room-mate spent most of her time at her boyfriend's apartment, so they could be alone. They had not been in the room five minutes before Ryker had pulled her into his arms.

Her kisses had been intoxicating.

"You have no idea how long I've wanted to kiss you," *Ryker whispered in her ear.*

"Kiss me again," she replied, lifting her mouth to accept the gentle kiss from his lips...

Ryker pushed away the memory of that night. There was no point in thinking about something that had happened years ago. He and Garland were both different people now.

Garland and Amya were over for dinner at Trina's.

"I love what you've done to your kitchen," Garland said, admiring Trina's walnut-colored floors. "I especially like this color granite you chose. The blue is pretty."

"Movie," Amya called.

Garland followed Trina and Amya out of the kitchen and into the family room. "What do you want to watch, sweetie?" Trina said in a cheerful voice.

"Pooh," Amya shouted.

"She's watched this movie at least twenty times," Trina said, glancing over to her.

"She loves it." Garland laughed.

While Trina turned on the DVD for Amya, Garland checked on the chicken in the oven.

"It's almost ready," she announced when Trina returned to the kitchen. "Thank you for inviting us for dinner."

"Anytime." Trina smiled.

Amya fussed when she was called to the dinner table ten minutes later. "Movie."

"It's time to eat," Garland said. "You can see the television from the table. C'mon, sweetheart."

"I can tell that this thing with the hospital is really bothering you," Trina said after they had finished eating and Amya was settled back in the family room. "Have you told your mom what's going on?"

"I told her yesterday and she took it well. I think it's because Ryker is involved." Garland sat her untouched glass of wine on the coffee table. "Trina, I can't lose my Amya. I never should've agreed to the DNA test."

"Honey, you need to know if you were given the right baby at birth. It would've haunted you for the rest of your life if you hadn't done the test."

"*Amya is my daughter.* I feel it in here," she said, her hand pressed to her chest. "I don't believe that my heart would lie to me."

"Then you have nothing to worry about when it comes to the DNA test," Trina said as she poured more wine in her glass. "It will only prove what you already know."

Garland nodded. "You're right. I don't know why I'm letting this upset me so."

"Because you're human."

"When they placed that little girl in my arms, I never knew I could love anyone so deeply. It was such an incredible feeling."

"Everything is going to work out, Garland. I believe it."

"The other thing that bothers me is that the DuGrandpres are involved. They have their millions and social standing in the community—they have the power to take Amya from me."

"But you have a relationship with Ryker," Trina pointed out. "He was Parker's best friend. You can talk to him. I believe the two of you can work something out if it becomes necessary."

Garland did not respond. Her thoughts were elsewhere.

"Garland?"

"Sorry, I was thinking about Ryker. When we were in college, I had a major crush on him."

"I never knew that."

"I didn't tell anyone."

"Did anything ever happen between you two?"

"We kissed one night and things got really intense but then Ryker backed off. He didn't want to upset Parker."

"So he's an honorable man."

Garland chuckled. "Too honorable, I thought at the time. I wanted him to be my one and only, but he obviously didn't feel the same." She shrugged. "Things worked out the way they were supposed to—he met and fell in love with someone else and I met a host of jerks."

They both laughed.

Garland shivered as she glanced around the room, the lighting a warm, flattering shade of gold against the muted mustard-colored walls. She leaned back into the luxuriously soft couch with a throw pillow on her lap.

"What are you thinking about right now?" Trina asked.

"How perfect my life was until recently. I feel like I took so much for granted."

"You didn't take anything for granted, Garland. Regardless of what the DNA tests say, you have a daughter. Just remember that."

Chapter 6

"Here we are again," Ryker said, approaching Garland. A couple of weeks had passed since their first meeting with the chief of staff and hospital attorneys.

The DNA results were in and Garland could feel fear spreading through her stomach.

They had been ushered into the chief of staff's office within minutes of their arrival.

Garland sat in one chair while Ryker took the other.

Her eyes filled with tears after the results were read.

Ryker uttered a groan before lashing out. "How could something like this happen in your hospital? How many times has this happened?"

Almost immediately, both she and Ryker were met with repeated apologies and regret for the anguish they naturally felt. "We have made changes to prevent something like this from ever happening again," Dr. Rainey stated. "We are putting electronic bracelets on both the mother and the child."

"I can't speak for Garland, but those words coming from you mean nothing to me," Ryker told them. "I could understand more if the babies were kidnapped and someone tried to take them out of the hospital. But our babies were switched right after they were born, in plain sight."

Ryker's intense gaze seemed to make the administrator nervous. Garland could almost smell the scent of a lawsuit coming from him. And she was considering filing one, as well.

She recognized the intense anxiety in the chief's gaze but refused to quiet his fears. The hospital deserved to pay for turning her world upside down. Though the truth was that she did not want or need their blood money. No amount of cash would ever make up for what had been done to her and Ryker or their daughters.

She rose to her feet. "There is nothing else to be said, I suppose."

"Miss Warner...please wait," the chief pleaded.

"For what?" she asked. "To reassure you that I won't file a lawsuit? If that's what you're expecting, I can't help you."

Dr. Rainey cleared his throat before saying, "Paige Ballard is a psychologist on staff here and she can assist—"

"Garland and I will find our own psychologist, if you don't mind. This situation will be worked out between us and out of the news. If I have to go to court to get a gag order, I will," Ryker interjected.

"I assure you, we would like to keep this quiet," Rainey quickly responded.

"I expect a press release to go out stating that none

of the children were switched," Ryker stated. "We do not want anyone to know about this. Do you understand me?"

Dr. Rainey nodded.

"Garland…" Ryker said once they were outside of the office.

"I'm sorry, but I can't do this right now," she said through exhaustion and dread. She then suddenly burst into tears. "I'm really sorry. I just need a moment."

"I thought maybe we could talk," Ryker stated.

"I can't believe this is happening," Garland said between sobs. "Amya's my daughter. *She's mine.*"

Acting purely out of instinct, he pulled her into his arms. "We will get through this."

"Our daughters…" His voice broke and Ryker stepped away from her. "Only we can decide on the future of our girls. Let me know when you're ready to talk."

"I will," she promised.

"For what it's worth, I understand everything you're feeling. My wife died and she never had the chance to hold her daughter. And I've just found out that neither have I."

Garland wiped away her tears. "This isn't fair to either of us."

They stared at each other.

"Ryker, I brought pictures of Amya," she said tentatively. Garland removed the envelope from her purse and handed it to him.

"She looks like Angela," he said. "Even her smile is like hers."

"Amya looks like her biological mother," Garland responded, stating what he wanted to say but would not.

"This must be even worse for you because your wife is gone."

Ryker looked up at her. "Our daughter was all I had left."

Garland heard the pain in his voice and felt the onset of panic. *He's going to want to take Amya from me,* she immediately thought.

"Kai looks like you," Ryker said, cutting into her thoughts. "It's funny, but when she makes certain expressions, I always thought she looked like Parker. It makes sense now because he's her uncle."

She and Ryker rode down in silence in the elevator. Garland was painfully conscious of his physical presence. She caught him glancing at her once or twice, but each time he looked away quickly. Right now, he seemed to be concentrating on the numbers over the elevator door.

He wants to get away from me as much as I want to get way from him, she thought.

When the elevator doors opened, Ryker stepped out of the way and allowed Garland to exit first.

"Where are you parked?" he asked.

"On the lower level of the parking deck. Why?"

"I want to make sure you're not accosted by media. I meant it when I said that I want to keep this out of the news."

Garland groaned. "Ryker, I hadn't thought of that."

"I'll walk you to your car."

"My car is right over there," she gestured. "I don't see anyone lurking around, so I'm sure I'll be fine. Thank you, Ryker."

The lines between his nose and mouth deepened. "We will talk soon."

She gave him a small nod.

Ryker bent his head in a stiff good-bye and stalked across the parking lot. Garland watched him leave. She did not want him to become an enemy. She would have to accommodate him, be his friend—do whatever was necessary to keep him from seeking custody—for the sake of the children they shared.

In a strange twist of fate, she and Ryker were tied to one another until Amya and Kai were grown.

Oblivious to the salt-scented breeze and the familiar sounds of the ocean, Garland stared at the envelope in her hand.

"Mommy, look at…" Amya tugged at her pant leg. "Look."

Her small hand cupped a mussel shell.

Garland smiled in delight and hugged her daughter. "It's so pretty."

"Yes," Amya responded.

For a moment, Garland watched as Amya wandered a few feet away to pick up a crab claw. She looked adorable in her denim shorts, pink shirt and sneakers and her dark curls pulled into a ponytail. Amya would always be *her* daughter.

Garland pulled her gaze from Amya, crouched on her heels and stared with intense fascination at the ground.

"How could this have happened," she whispered. She had been awake during her painful labor and delivery. She had begun hemorrhaging, which prevented her from seeing her daughter for the first few hours after she had given birth. But when the nurse had placed Amya in her arms, Garland fell completely in love with the newborn.

She glanced up to find her daughter in the exact same

spot. Amya loved collecting seashells and odd-colored rocks along the shore, just as Garland had when she was a little girl growing up on the island.

She kept fingering the yellow official-looking envelope. Garland inhaled deeply and released the air slowly before pulling out a single sheet of paper, unfolding it. Even with the evidence in her trembling hands, she still found it hard to believe.

Her heart pounded loudly and her vision misted with tears. Garland rushed over to Amya, embracing her. "It's time to go home, sweetie. C'mon—let's get out of here."

"Mommy?"

Swallowing her sadness, she forced a smile. "It's almost time for dinner."

"Shicken nuggets," Amya suggested with the smile of an angel. "Fench fries."

"You know what?" Garland responded. "Chicken nuggets and French fries sound good to me." She hugged the toddler and whispered, "I want you to know that I love you very much."

"I wuv you, too," she murmured. "Gimme kiss…"

Garland planted a gentle kiss on her daughter's lips.

Feeling numb, she turned her back on the ocean waves and took Amya's small hand.

Garland's whole world was her daughter and now that world had become a nightmare.

Ryker's surroundings suddenly seemed to evaporate as he tossed on his desk the sheet of paper containing the DNA results, proving that the little girl who had been placed in his arms was not the same one his wife had carried for nine months. According to the document, Kai was not his child.

He shook his head. *How could this happen?*

He was focused on only one thought: regardless of whose blood ran through Kai's veins, she was still his daughter and the fierceness of his love could not be diminished. He would never give her up.

Yet his heart yearned to see his biological daughter. There was no way he could *not* be a part of her life.

A knock on the door cut into his thoughts as his cousin entered the room.

"Are you okay, Ryker?" Jordin asked.

"When I went into that hospital, I expected to leave with the proof that Kai is my daughter."

"What are you saying?"

Ryker's response was interrupted by his parent's arrival.

"What happened?" they asked in unison.

"Kai is not my daughter," he stated, his eyes filling with tears and his throat aching with defeat. "She's not mine."

"No," Rochelle gasped.

Her husband embraced her. "I can't believe it."

Jordin walked over to Ryker and placed a comforting hand on his shoulder. "I'm so sorry."

"So what do you intend to do about this situation?" Rochelle said as she wiped away her tears.

"I'm not sure," Ryker confessed. "Two innocent girls are involved."

"Both of whom are your daughters," Jordin interjected.

"They are also Garland's daughters."

"They belong with you," Rochelle blurted. "You can offer them a wonderful and financially secure life."

"This isn't about who has the most money, Mom,"

Ryker uttered in a low, tormented voice. "Love is what a child needs more."

"I'm sure Aunt Rochelle didn't mean it that way," Jordin said.

"Son, why don't you take a couple of days just to think about things?" his father suggested. "Right now everyone is too emotional."

"I can cover your cases for you," Jordin offered.

Ryker nodded. "Okay, thanks. I'll need to call Angela's parents."

He picked up the telephone as soon as he was alone in his office. He probably should've already told his in-laws what was going on so they could have absorbed the shock slowly, but he hadn't wanted to alarm them unnecessarily. Kai was all they had left of their daughter. Now he had to tell them about Amya.

"Mom," he said when Edna Harvey answered the phone.

"Ryker, hello. I was just thinking about you and Kai. Are you still planning to come for a visit later this summer?"

"Something has happened," he began. At her sharp intake of breath, he instantly regretted his words. "Kai is fine. I didn't mean to scare you."

"Oh, thank goodness," she murmured.

"Is Dad there with you?"

"He's here," Edna replied. "Ryker, what's going on?"

"Ask him to pick up one of the other phone extensions. I want to tell you both at the same time."

"Oh…okay…"

Ryker hated having to do this, but he needed to tell them the truth.

Edna returned to the phone. "Ralph and I are both on the line. Please tell us what's happened."

"The thing is…on the day Kai was born, there was a mix-up at the hospital."

"What do you mean, Ryker?" Her voice trembled.

"Kai is not my biological daughter. She is not the baby Angela gave birth to that day."

"Ryker, I'm afraid I don't understand," Ralph interjected. "What are you saying, son?"

"A nurse somehow switched the babies and I brought the wrong one home."

"Are you sure?" Edna asked.

"We had DNA tests done," he responded. "It's impossible for me to have fathered Kai. The good news is that the woman who has my daughter and I have met. She is actually the sister of my old best friend, Parker."

"You'll be bringing her home then?" Edna asked. "Angela's little girl."

"Mom, we're taking it slowly," he explained. "This woman loves Amya—that's her name. I understand because I love Kai."

"We all love Kai," she agreed. "But Angela's daughter can't be raised by someone else. I won't allow it and neither can you, Ryker. It's not right."

"Mom, what do you want me to do?" he questioned. "I am not willing to give up Kai. I'm the only parent she's ever known."

"But our granddaughter…"

"I hope that you will continue to think of Kai that way."

"Angela was all we had," she said. "Our only child."

"Why don't I arrange for you all to meet Amya as soon as possible?" he suggested. "Garland is a nice person and I know she'll understand. I can't imagine her being unwilling to involve you in Amya's life."

"My daughter never would've named her daughter Amya."

"I think it's a pretty name," Ryker said. "Mom, we have to take this slow for the sake of the girls."

"I suppose so," Edna mumbled. "But I can't believe that you're going to just leave your own flesh and blood with a complete stranger."

"I agree," Ralph chimed in.

"I'm the stranger to Amya," he reminded his in-laws. "Would you really wrench her from the only home she's ever known?"

"No," Edna answered after a moment. "We just want to meet her, Ryker."

"And you will," he promised, "but you have to be patient."

He ended the call a few minutes later. His in-laws would not meet Amya anytime soon because he did not trust them not to tell her that they were her grandparents.

Ryker packed up his laptop and left his office filled with anger and an intense frustration churning in his stomach. Kai had just lost her grandparents—he was sure of it. Once they saw Amya, they would immediately gravitate to her.

He felt an unhappiness he had never known.

Chapter 7

The dream came every night.

Garland was searching desperately for her daughter. First, she'd be on the beach reading a book when she'd look up suddenly and realize she did not see her.

"Amya!" she'd begin calling. "Amya, where are you?"

She'd leap to her feet and spin in every direction, screaming repeatedly, "Amya!"

Garland would begin stumbling toward the water, the hearty roar of the surf filling her ears.

Then she'd realize that she was no longer on the beach but in Charleston, running up the sidewalk and searching frantically for her daughter. The sound from nearby traffic would frighten her. People passing would ignore her pleas for help. Then she would see Kai teetering near the street. The overwhelming shock of helplessness would hold her immobile.

She'd call out Kai's name but realize with horror that her flesh-and-blood daughter did not know who she was. She would not remember meeting her at the boutique. "Stay there," Garland would scream. "Please don't move. I'm going to help you."

The little girl would look scared and would back away as Garland neared. "Nooo," she'd shout.

Garland always shot up in bed just as Kai stepped off the curb. She would then burst into tears, feeling bereft and desolate and her body trembling and shuddering.

Tonight she pulled herself together quickly enough to check on Amya before returning to her room.

Wrapped in a cocoon of anguish, Garland padded barefoot into the bathroom and splashed cold water on her face. She then stared hopelessly at herself in the mirror. Her misery was so acute that it was actual physical pain.

Ryker leaned back in the leather office chair. He rubbed his eyes, which burned from lack of sleep. He'd woken up wanting to believe that yesterday had been nothing but a bad dream.

Pain stabbed now, causing Ryker to rub his chest. Kai was not his biological daughter. He searched every inch of her angelic face, looking for another answer but then he shook his head. It no longer mattered because DNA didn't lie. The darling little girl he had brought home from the hospital belonged to Garland.

Ryker could not wait to meet the daughter he shared with Angela. He shuddered at the reality that he had never met his own little girl.

A shred of guilt snaked down his spine. He had been oblivious to the baby switch. He should have paid more attention when his daughter was born. This was something else he had screwed up. If Angela were alive, she would be furious with him.

Ryker vowed he would find a way to make it up to both of the girls one day. He did not know a thing about girly secrets, teen crushes, makeup or any of those things that were important to girls, but he was willing to learn. He would never abandon Kai or Amya.

How would Garland fit into his life? The question had popped into his head more than once throughout the night. But Ryker still had no answer.

It was complicated.

Ryker knew that she loved Amya with her entire being. He felt the same way about Kai. They could not just switch the girls—he was sure that Garland would never go for that. And he did not believe it was the way to go, either.

There was a time when he'd considered a relationship with Garland but convinced himself that it would be wrong, especially because her brother was his best friend. Under different circumstances, he could probably have appreciated the irony that he was now bound to her forever through Amya and Kai.

In a way, Ryker was relieved that Garland was the one who had raised his daughter. He knew that his daughter was loved and well cared for. He also knew that they would be able to find common ground because of their connection to Parker.

Hearing his mother's voice in the hallway outside of his office snapped him out of his contemplation. Ryker knew exactly what she would want to happen—both girls to be raised by him. In truth, he rather liked the idea as well, but he knew that Garland would never agree to that arrangement.

The only alternative left was to grant visitation rights to Garland and vice versa. Although Ryker could live with this option, he would have preferred to be a full-time father to both Kai and Amya.

A knock on the door pulled him out of his reverie.

"Come in," he said.

As Jordin walked in, he smiled at her. "You are just the person I want to see. I need some legal advice regarding family law and I don't want to discuss this with my mother."

"Miss Warner," Ryker greeted when she walked into his office the following day.

"Please…we're way past formality," Garland responded, taking a seat in one of the visitor chairs facing his desk. "I'm sure you know why I'm here."

Ryker seemed mildly surprised by her words. "Let's talk."

"I'd like to spend time with my daughter," she blurted and then shook her head sadly. "This is still so awkward."

He agreed. "I still don't believe this is really happening. When the news first broke—I kept telling myself that it had nothing to do with my daughter."

"I felt the same way," Garland admitted. "I'm sure you're just as anxious to meet Amya as I am to get to know Kai."

"I am," he admitted. "A chance reunion and now our lives are suddenly intertwined."

"This is not easy on either one of us. It's going to take some time before we're all comfortable."

He did not respond.

"I would like for you and Kai to come over for dinner this evening," Garland stated. "The girls can get to know each another and we can talk." She wanted to have their initial meeting on her turf. She would feel more comfortable in her own home.

Ryker met her gaze. "I agree that we need to talk about the children and their future."

"Why don't you and Kai come over tonight around seven?"

He nodded. "We'll be there."

Garland rose to her feet. "I don't want to take up any more of your time."

"I appreciate you coming by, Garland," Ryker responded with a smile.

"I'll see you tonight."

Her visit left him in a good mood. To his surprise, Garland was ready to connect with him and Kai. He was also anxious to meet Amya but did not want to push her before she was ready. Garland coming to him paved the way for him to finally meet his daughter.

Chapter 8

Garland's invitation to dinner made it easier on Ryker. He had been ready for this meeting from the moment they received the DNA results, but he had not wanted to pressure her.

Although they'd been thrown together under rocky circumstances, Garland was willing to work with him toward a viable solution. In her eyes and in the firming of her luscious lips, he could see that she was not happy about any of this—and she was not the only one twisted into knots emotionally.

We will find a way to make this work, he silently vowed.

Ryker was actually looking forward to spending the evening with Garland and the girls. He could not wait to meet Amya. He hoped that the two girls became close friends. He was not worried about his relationship with Garland. They had always gotten along well.

Most of the women he had known over the years enjoyed being around him because of his family's wealth, but Garland and Angela had been different. Garland had always been able to find beauty in the most unlikely places. She had never been interested in high society or making connections through him.

She still managed to affect him, cut through his defenses and take him to a place he was not used to finding himself. Ryker had learned to control his emotions after Angela's death. That would come in handy now—it was important not to break down in front of Kai. He was her father, her protector. He had to be strong for her.

He knew that with Garland, it would not be so easy. She had always been able to affect him in ways no other woman could, including Angela.

This is about the girls, he reminded himself. Amya and Kai had to come first. Ryker was not ready for a relationship with anyone because he needed to focus on raising both Kai and Amya. Regardless of the mixed emotions Garland drew out of him, he would never act on them.

After setting up the dinner date with Ryker, Garland made her way toward the double doors in the reception area of the law firm.

"Miss Warner?"

She turned around, surprised to find Ryker's mom standing there. "Mrs. DuGrandpre, it's good to see you."

"What are you doing here?"

"I came by to see Ryker. I invited him and Kai over for dinner." Garland had no idea why she mentioned that they were planning to have dinner together. She regretted it the instant the words were out of her mouth.

"I see," Rochelle responded, her arms folded across her chest. "You're certainly not wasting any time, are you?"

"I don't know what you mean," Garland stated as calmly as she could manage.

"I don't know what you're planning, but I want to be clear. We are not going to let you yank Kai out of our arms, Miss Warner. We are not going to let you keep my biological granddaughter away from us, either."

"That's not what I'm trying to do." Garland shifted her purse to her other hand, imposing an iron control on herself. "You don't know me, Mrs. DuGrandpre, but Ryker does. Your son and I are going to find a solution that works best for both girls."

"I hope you will consider the psychological implications for these children—"

"They are our first priority. Now if you will excuse me, I need to get back to the boutique," Garland said cutting her off.

"I'm looking forward to getting to know my *other* granddaughter," Rochelle said pointedly. "You have a good day, Miss Warner."

She walked away before Garland could respond.

As she headed to her car, she fought hard against the tears she refused to let fall. During the drive back to Edisto Island, Garland considered how grateful she was that Ryker was nothing like his mother.

Trina was waiting for Garland at the boutique when she arrived.

"I came by to check on you."

She clenched her jaw to kill the sob in her throat. "I can't begin to tell you how I'm feeling right now."

"Did something happen?"

"I invited Ryker and Kai over to the house for dinner this evening."

"That is a good thing, right?"

Garland nodded. "His mother stopped me when I was leaving his office. She gave me the impression that they want both girls."

"They can't keep you from your own daughter," Trina stated.

"But what about Amya?" she questioned. "I know she's not the one I gave birth to, but I can't just let her go."

"I can't imagine what you're going through, sweetie."

"Do you think I should get some legal advice?"

"Definitely. You need to be prepared for whatever the DuGrandpre family may have in mind."

Ryker and Kai arrived at Garland and Amya's home early.

He parked his SUV at the curb outside of her house. It was just as he'd imagined—flower beds crowded with color and scent.

"Look it," Kai murmured, pointing at the flowers.

"It's pretty, isn't it?"

Kai smiled and nodded.

Ryker's gaze fixed on Garland as she stood on the porch. It took them only seconds to join her there and then follow her into the house.

Her house was small, but warm and cozy. She had sprinkled a solid collection of pieces by local artists around the living room. An olive-colored sofa and two overstuffed chairs sat opposite each other in front of a stone fireplace.

Kai clung to Ryker's leg, and he noticed that Garland

was struggling not to stare at the little girl. He knew she did not want to make her uncomfortable.

"Sweetie," he said, swallowing hard. "This is my friend Miss Garland. Do you remember meeting her at the store where you got your princess bear?"

Garland could not seem to tear her eyes away from Kai. "Do you remember me?"

Kai nodded. In a sudden bout of shyness, she buried her face in his thigh.

Garland seemed to understand that the little girl needed to time to get comfortable, so she said, "Amya, our guests are here. Come say hello."

"Okay, Mommy," Amya answered from the kitchen.

"I have a little girl who wants to meet you," Garland said. "Her name is Amya."

"Mya," Kai whispered.

Ryker took a ragged breath when Amya came running into the room. She glanced up at him and broke into a grin. "Hello," she greeted.

"Hello, little one," he murmured. "You must be Amya."

"Yes," she answered in a low voice. "Me."

Amya caught sight of Kai peeking around Ryker's thigh and walked over to her. "Hello."

Kai waved and then hid her face against Ryker's trouser leg once again.

Amya looked back at Garland.

"She's shy, sweetie," Garland explained.

Amya then turned and ran off.

"Is she upset?" he asked.

Garland shook her head as she gazed at Kai.

Amya returned with two bears. She held one out to Kai. "I share."

Kai walked from behind him and accepted the bear. "Tank you."

He turned toward Garland, meeting her gaze. "This is incredible. I have pictures of Angela as a child. She is the exact image of her mother."

"She has a lot of you in her, as well," Garland said, her eyes shimmering with amusement and devilment. "Look at her ears. They stick out a little, just like yours."

Ryker laughed. "You would notice that." He remembered how she used to tease him about his ears whenever he and Parker gave her a hard time.

"Amya, why don't you take Kai to your room?" Garland suggested. "You can show her your playhouse."

He and Garland followed a few minutes later.

The room, decorated in pink and white, was filled with bits of chatter and laughter along with a bookshelf loaded with books, a chair filled with stuffed animals, a basket of dress-up clothes and a canopy bed.

"She's so beautiful," Garland murmured as she watched Kai and Amya playing.

"They both are," Ryker responded.

"Is she with a nanny all day?"

He shook his head. "She goes to day care during the week."

"Really," Garland murmured. "I'm surprised you don't have a nanny or au pair."

"Do you really think of me in that way?" he asked her. "I don't want someone else raising my daughter." After a moment passed he said, "I wasn't referring to you."

Garland chewed on her bottom lip. "Where do you suggest we go from here? Should we get lawyers involved and let the courts mandate their futures?" She glanced over at Amya. "You can't have her, you know.

She is my daughter and I love her dearly. I'm her whole world and she is mine."

Ryker's mouth twisted. "It would seem that we have this in common. I'd fight to the death for Kai. If you think that you're going to raise both girls, you're wrong. Nobody is taking her from me, so you might as well put that right out of your mind." Ryker eyed his daughter. "On Kai's nightstand is a picture of Angela. She knows that her mommy lives in heaven. I'm not sure how to explain this situation to a two-year-old. Right now, she knows you as Amya's mom."

"Maybe all this will be less scary once they know us, Ryker."

"Maybe," he responded. "For now, we will just hang out as friends."

"Something like that," Garland stated.

"Kai is going to like coming over here to visit. She loves spending the day at the beach. I guess it comes natural to her."

Garland smiled in response, then said, "Let's settle the two girls in the family room in front of the television while I get dinner."

"They are so beautiful," Ryker murmured as he watched the two girls get comfortable on the couch.

"Moovie…" Amya said.

"Would you like to watch *The Lorax*?" Garland asked.

"Yessh," Kai responded with a grin and a nod.

"This is Amya's favorite movie."

"Kai loves it, as well."

She met his gaze. "Dinner is just about ready. Why don't you join the girls while I set everything out?"

"I'll help you in the kitchen," Ryker told her. "We can talk."

"I have a confession to make," Garland stated as they entered the kitchen. "I never really pictured you as a father. I always thought you would turn out to be a bachelor for life."

He broke into a grin. "I really didn't think about parenthood until Angela told me she was pregnant. It was something we had talked about, but then we found out that she was carrying Kai…" Ryker paused a moment. "I'm sorry. She was carrying Amya."

"It's okay," Garland assured him. "This would be a whole lot more awkward if we were complete strangers. If this had to happen—I'm glad it was with you, Ryker. I know I sound crazy."

"No, I get it."

Ten minutes later, the table was laden with a chicken and rice casserole, green beans and yeast rolls.

Ryker broke into a grin. "You remembered how much I loved your mom's chicken and rice casserole."

"It's all she ever cooked whenever you had dinner with us."

He noted there were two booster chairs at the table and his expression clouded, eyes going narrow. "When did you get the second one?"

"I've had it for months," Garland responded. "I take it with us whenever we eat out."

"Oh." Ryker had wrongly assumed she was already preparing for Kai's place in her life. Thankfully, she missed the assumption. He did not want the night to end on a sour note.

Chapter 9

After dinner, they sat down in the family room where the girls had already settled. Kai had warmed up to Amya and the two played and laughed as they watched TV.

"Amya looks so much like Angela. It's so amazing to me." Ryker glanced over at Garland. "I wish you two could've met."

"She sounds like she was a wonderful person."

"Why didn't you come to my wedding? I invited both you and your mother."

"Mom wasn't up to it," Garland said. "It was one of her low days. I'm sure it was a beautiful ceremony."

"It was," he responded, then changed the subject. "Garland, I have to be honest with you. I want to be a part of my daughter's life. I've spoken to psychologists who have suggested that the girls are young enough to adapt if we switch them."

"I'll be just as honest with you," Garland responded. "I don't want to switch children, Ryker. I feel like both Kai and Amya are my daughters. I may have given birth to Kai, but Amya is just as much my child as Kai. I'm sure you must feel the same way."

He nodded. "I do, but if we don't want to switch them, then what should we do? We are going to have to come up with a solution."

"I know," Garland said. "But for now, I just want the girls to get to know one another. And I haven't seen you in years, so we need to get to know each other all over again."

"I don't think it will be too difficult," he said with a grin. "I haven't changed much."

"Well, I'm afraid I'm not the same little girl you used to know."

"I was thinking that we could try and let the girls spend the weekends together," Ryker stated. "I know that you work some Saturdays, but I don't mind watching them both on those days. I could drop Kai off some Sundays so that you can spend time with her."

"It may be better to start off with short visits at first," Garland interjected. "Amya hasn't gone on playdates for more than a couple of hours at a time. She has spent the night with Trina, but she's her godmother, so she knows her well."

"She's used to preschool, right?" he asked.

"Yes, but I still prefer to start off with just a few hours first."

"Okay."

"Does it only have to be on the weekends?" Garland inquired. "I'm off on Wednesdays and the store is closed on Sundays as you know. I'd like to try and meet for dinner on Wednesdays, if possible."

"I could take some Wednesdays off or leave work early," Ryker said thoughtfully. "Kai would probably be thrilled to stay home from school one day a week. Also, it might be a good idea for us to see a counselor," Ryker suggested.

"Why do we need to see a counselor?" Garland questioned.

"He or she can give us advice in building relationships with our biological children."

"I don't think we need to see someone for that," Garland stated. "I think what we're doing now is fine. I want the girls to know us on their own terms."

"Sounds good to me." She pointed to his empty glass. "Would you like more tea?"

"Yes. Thank you."

Grabbing the glass, Garland rose to her feet and headed to the kitchen.

Ryker turned when he heard her singing softly as she retrieved the pitcher of iced tea from the refrigerator.

"Kai does that," Ryker stated when she returned.

Garland handed him the glass of iced tea. "What?"

"She sings, especially when she's playing and sometimes when she's eating."

"Really?"

Ryker nodded. "It's amazing to see just how much she is like you."

Garland sat down beside him. "I've noticed recently that when Amya makes certain expressions, she looks like you."

"It's so good to see you again," Ryker said. He reached out, covering her hand with his own.

"I figured you'd forgotten all about me. It's not like we were really *friends*."

"We had our own relationship outside of Parker," Ryker uttered, surprised by her words.

Garland's gaze snapped to his. "You only tolerated your best friend's little sister and you know it."

"You have to know that's not true." Ryker paused a second. "Do you want to talk about that night?"

"Maybe we should clear the air."

"Garland, I want you to know that I would never disrespect you. I had been drinking that night and I got carried away."

"Ryker, you didn't ravish me or anything. We just kissed and…"

"We almost ended up in bed together."

"We didn't, so there was no harm done."

"If you weren't my best friend's sister, things could have been very different for us," Ryker confessed. "But because of Parker, I couldn't cross that line with you."

"As I said, there was no harm done, so now we can forget about that night. No point on dwelling in the past when we have so much to look forward to in the future," Garland stated.

"Mommy, applesoys," Amya said. "Please."

"Would you like some applesauce, Kai?"

"Yessh," she responded. "Abblesauce."

Garland met Ryker's gaze and smiled. "She is so adorable."

"Come to the table," she instructed the toddlers.

They followed her without an utter of protest.

"Dayee," Kai called out. "Look it."

He smiled. "I see. Eat your applesauce like a big girl."

"Daddee," Amya repeated with a huge grin on her face. She pointed at Ryker and said it once more. "Daddee."

Her words clearly caught Garland off guard because her steps came to a sudden halt. Her gaze mirrored Ryker's surprised expression.

"I think she's just testing the word out," Garland said in a low voice when she returned to her seat.

"Does she have a relationship with her...father?"

Garland met his gaze. "No, I was artificially inseminated, Ryker."

"I suppose that makes things a little less complicated."

"I guess," she mumbled.

"It's fine if she wants to call me Daddy," Ryker said after a slight pause. "After all, I am her father."

"It's just very awkward for me," Garland confessed. "I really wish..."

"That this hadn't happened," he finished her sentence.

"I shouldn't say that," she said finally. "Because then I wouldn't have Amya and she's my life. I guess I wish that that nurse had just taken this to her grave. Then we would have never found out."

"Unless something happened where medical attention was needed," Ryker pointed out. "I think it would have been worse to find out in a situation like that." He covered her hand with his own. "We are going to work this out," Ryker assured her. "I know that we will do what's best for our girls."

"Definitely. Oh, I ran into your mother after I left your office earlier today," Garland stated. "I have to say that she's a bit intense."

He chuckled. "She can be whenever it comes to something she's passionate about. My mother is a brilliant lawyer and an advocate for children."

"Does she still specialize in family law?" she asked.

"Yes."

"I find that admirable," Garland stated. "Unfortunately, we need people like your mother to protect children from their families or others out to harm them. How does she feel about this situation?"

"My parents love Kai and I know that they are also going to love Amya. In fact, my family can't wait to meet her. Angela's parents also want to meet Amya, but I told them that they might have to wait."

Garland smiled with obvious difficulty. "Thank you."

"We are the only two people who can make decisions for our children."

"I'm relieved you feel this way," she said. "I don't want to have to deal with your entire family right now."

"I wouldn't put you through that, Garland," Ryker said, the sincerity evident in his voice.

Garland tried desperately to ignore the sizzle of heat that shot up her arm and burned in the center of her chest. She struggled to disregard the feelings he ignited in her, especially because he clearly was not interested in her.

After the girls finished eating, Ryker decided it was time for their visit to wind down.

"What are you doing on Wednesday?" he asked.

"I don't have any plans, but I was hoping you and Kai could join us for a day at the beach."

Ryker broke into a grin. "It's a date."

She smiled and nodded.

* * *

"Why can't I get Ryker out of my head?" Garland whispered as she picked up the television remote. Ryker and Kai had been gone for at least half an hour. Garland had resolved to bottle up whatever feelings she had for him—she needed to be in control. Besides, he had made it clear that he would never cross any lines with her because of Parker.

A small part of Garland blamed her swirling emotions on the fact that he was the father of her daughter. In college, she used to dream about what life with Ryker would be like but never once considered that their futures would ever intersect. She was a realist. She knew that a girl like her would never fit in the world of a Du-Grandpre.

Garland still had mixed feelings about Amya calling Ryker *Daddy*. It was as if her little heart knew what her mind was too young to understand.

"I can't lose her," Garland whispered to the empty room.

Images of Garland filled Ryker's thoughts all night long. The way she lifted her chin when she was adamant about something, the sexy way she fingered her short curls and the way she smiled—it was electrifying.

Ryker could still smell the light fragrance she wore and envision her maxi dress draped lovingly over her curves. Her short hair was a mass of curls, making her look years younger than she was. Ryker tried not to, but he could not help noticing her full breasts and curvy shape. In college he had been very attracted to her. He still was, Ryker realized in dismay.

Don't go there, he told himself. Things were already sensitive enough between them. But Garland made him feel things he had not felt since the death of his wife. She sparked long-buried flames of desire within. With Angela gone, he had suppressed his needs, choosing instead to focus on Kai.

Ryker groaned in protest when sleep continued to elude him. Was it going to be this way every time he spent time with Garland?

He had changed positions at least three times in the past thirty minutes. Finally, he sat up in bed, reached for the remote and turned on the television.

A show about a father and daughter caught his attention, bringing to mind just how blessed he was to have not one but two beautiful daughters. In time, he hoped to assure Garland that he would be a great father to Amya and Kai. He did not want to push too soon because they'd agreed that the toddlers needed time to bond with their biological parents and with each other. He and Garland both had decided to hold off on making any decisions for now.

Ryker was impatient, though. He was ready to have Kai's bedroom renovated to include twin beds and another set of bookshelves to store Amya's stuffed animals. He wanted to bring his daughter home. He wanted to introduce her to his family. But Ryker knew he first needed to seal his bond with Amya before introducing others into her life.

His mother was just as impatient. It had been her suggestion to seek out a counselor. Ryker would do things Garland's way for now, but if this did not work, then he would give her no choice but to do things his way. He was thrilled that Amya and Kai had taken to each other, although they were very different. Amya was bubbly and very outgoing, whereas Kai was more reserved and quiet.

He knew Garland well enough to know that she would not allow him to raise the girls alone. She loved them fiercely. Ryker had no doubts about her parenting skills.

Ryker thought back to earlier when he had inhaled her soft scent as she walked past him. From the moment they'd first met, Garland had made an impression on him, one he found disturbing at times. His skin grew tighter with every glance.

Get a grip, he reminded himself. Ryker rationalized that his recent feelings stemmed from not being with a woman since Angela's death. He tried to convince himself that the sensuality lingering in the air was out of loneliness.

Money.

Everything about Ryker's house reinforced the fact that he had money—plenty of it.

What chance would she have if she had to take him on for custody? Garland pushed the thought out of her mind.

She admired the flower beds filled with hostas and other shade-loving plants.

Garland opened the rear passenger door and unbuckled Amya's seatbelt. "C'mon, sweetie. Your daddy and Kai are inside waiting for us."

"Daddee."

They had not reached the front door before Ryker strolled out with Kai holding his hand. He wore a pair of jeans and a polo shirt. He looked quite handsome, Garland thought. She was more comfortable around him when he was not dressed in a suit and looking all lawyerlike.

"Mya," Kai murmured.

Amya grinned and rushed over to Kai, touching the bow in Kai's hair. "Pretty."

Ryker's gaze met Garland's. "Come on inside."

Inside the ornately designed door, a marble entry led to a large living room with a wall of windows, gleaming hardwood floors and a stunning set of comfortable-looking leather furniture. Modern art on the walls and a few sculptures lent character to a room that might otherwise have been considered too tame for Garland's tastes.

"You have a really beautiful home."

"Thank you," he said. "Would you like a tour?"

"Sure."

"Kai, why don't you take Amya to the playroom?" Ryker coaxed. "I'll start a movie for you two to watch."

"Mommy, you no go?" Amya asked.

"No, I'm not leaving, sweetie," she responded gently. "I'll be right here."

During her tour, Garland caught glimpses into other rooms throughout Ryker's home. One held a seventy-inch big-screen television and state-of-the-art stereo equipment with theater-style seating; she also spotted a formal dining room and an office filled with floor-to-ceiling bookshelves.

She found Kai and Amya in a young girl's fantasy room. Shelves of books, dolls and stuffed animals covered every wall except for the one with the windows. A pink Ferrari sat parked in front of a huge Barbie Dreamhouse.

"This room is a little girl's dream come true."

"It's probably too much, but I just wanted to make her happy," he explained. "I wanted everything to be perfect for Kai."

"Just love her," Garland advised. "Nothing is more important than love."

He looked deep in thought. "You're right."

"It doesn't hurt to spoil them a little, though," she whispered. "Especially when they're so sweet."

Ryker's gaze moved to the generous swell of her breasts and he almost groaned at the lurch of sexual desire. A few minutes with Garland and she had triggered feelings he thought were long gone.

"I didn't want to ruin your impression of me by making dinner...hence the pizza," he explained.

She broke into a grin. "I already know that you suck at cooking. Remember when you tried to make s'mores in the microwave?"

Ryker laughed at the memory. "It took me two days to clean that thing out."

"Didn't you know that you're not supposed to put foil in the microwave?"

"I learned the hard way. Parker actually bought a new one that Christmas. He said we couldn't keep using that one because it never worked right after that day."

"I bought the microwave for you guys," Garland announced. "I got tired of you all coming over to my place and eating me out of house and home."

"You could cook," Ryker said. "We couldn't, and cereal three times a day wasn't cutting it."

"Oh please...girls were always trying to buy you dinner or whatever you wanted."

Ryker shook his head. "You got that wrong. Girls wanted *me* to pay for everything. They expected me to take them shopping and to expensive restaurants. I got tired of explaining that my parents had money but I was just a college student like everyone else."

"Maybe you should've left the BMW at home," Garland responded.

"You were never like those other girls."

"I don't impress easily. I never have been that way."

"That's what I liked about your brother. He accepted me for me. Our friendship was real."

Chapter 10

The following week, Ryker and Kai joined Garland and Amya for dinner on Edisto Island. Things were working out nicely, but for how long, Ryker wondered.

He wanted the girls to go to preschool together. It was hard to be away from one daughter while having to assure the other one that they would see Garland and Amya soon.

He considered asking Garland to move to Charleston but changed his mind. It was not fair to ask her to just pack up and move just for him. Her business was on the island. It was not that huge of a drive, he reasoned.

"You've been quiet all evening," Garland said, taking a seat beside him. "Long day at the office?"

"No, I was thinking about the girls," Ryker responded. "Kai gets so upset whenever she is away from you and Amya."

"Amya is the same way," Garland stated. "She loves sleeping with Kai. Lately I've been having to stay with her until she falls asleep."

Ryker shrugged. "I thought this was the best thing for them."

"What else can we do at this point?"

"I don't know," he responded. "I've considered asking you to move to Charleston, but I'm not sure that would be the solution."

"I'd be much closer, but it's not like we'd be in the same house," Garland stated.

Ryker had not meant to have this conversation with her tonight, but maybe it was best that they face possible problems before they arose. "I know we didn't want to rush anything…" he started. "But we definitely need to consider thinking about the future."

Her eyes were huge and beautiful and had darkened with apprehension. "What exactly do you mean by thinking ahead? Are you talking about months or years? Things aren't entirely smooth, but they are going well, I think."

Ryker resisted the urge to shift under her probing gaze. "I just want to make sure the girls are happy."

"They are happy, but I need to know something from you, Ryker," she said. "Are you okay with this arrangement? I need to know the truth."

"It seems to be the best we can do for now." he responded. "I'm glad that we have reconnected, Garland. There was a piece missing and I'm now realizing that part was you. I have to be honest with you, Garland. I've missed you as much as I've missed your brother."

She and Ryker spent the next hour watching TV and laughing with the girls. When Kai began to yawn and become cranky, he decided it was time for them to head back to Charleston.

It was also Amya's bedtime.

Garland walked Ryker to the door. He carried Kai in his arms.

"I'll see you soon," she told Kai. "I'll give you a call, Ryker," she said as she closed the door behind them.

Ten minutes later, her doorbell rang.

Garland stepped aside to let Trina enter the house. "I thought maybe you changed your mind about coming over."

"Did I just see Ryker DuGrandpre leaving here?" When Garland nodded, she added, "How's it going between you two?"

"Fine," Garland responded.

At that moment Amya ran out of her bedroom, her eyes searching. "Daddee…"

"He's not here, honey. He and Kai went home."

"No," Amya responded.

Garland picked up her daughter. "You'll see him on Saturday."

Trina met Garland's gaze. "Did she say what I think she said?"

She nodded. "Amya adores him. When Ryker was over here, she completely ignored me. I guess she has really been missing out on a father figure in her life."

"Kai looks like you from what you've told me," Trina stated. "She is a miniature you."

Garland broke into a smile. "She's so smart. Trina, you should see the two of them together. They get along so well."

"Like siblings."

She nodded. "I'd like to raise them as sisters."

"What does Ryker want to do?"

"We haven't really talked about it in depth," Garland replied. "Our focus has been allowing the girls to get to know one another. We both feel it is for the best. Amya hates to see them leave. She gets so upset."

The truth was that Garland hated the thought of leaving Amya with Ryker—not being there to see what happened, what she said and what they did.

"So, do you think you and Ryker will reconnect?" Trina questioned. "He's a handsome man and a successful lawyer."

"That's not where my head is at, Trina."

"I don't know why not," she stated. "That man is near perfection."

Garland laughed. "Then maybe you should date him."

"I don't think he's interested in me—Garland."

"Ryker is just being nice, Trina. Don't read any more into it," Garland stated. "I'm certainly not going to, although he did invite me to be his date at his parent's anniversary party next weekend. It's only because of Kai and Amya, though."

"Or he might actually want to spend some time with you, Garland."

"His marriage will always be a wall between us."

"His wife is dead," Trina said gently. "Ryker may still love her, but she is no longer here in this world."

"Ryker is still grieving for Angela and is still very much in love with her. Trust me. There is no room in his heart for anyone else except his daughters."

* * *

Kai cried during the first ten minutes of the drive back to Charleston. The tears became whimpers until she fell asleep.

Ryker's mind raced, jumping from one idea to another, never settling on one. Garland still haunted him. He was not able to get her out of his mind, and with that came guilt. He felt like he was cheating on Angela, although nothing sexual had happened between them. He had not even kissed her, but he thought about it often.

He tried unsuccessfully to convince himself that she was just another woman, but he knew that was a lie. Garland was special. She was not a woman on the prowl or a superficial socialite.

The years had been good to Garland. Her curves were more pronounced now that she had given birth. Her gorgeous hazel eyes had a hypnotic quality to them.

Garland was more than beautiful and sexy. She was also very intelligent. Despite her family background, she was determined to make a success out of her life. He admired her hunger and motivation to turn things around for herself.

He was proud of her accomplishments. Ryker glanced heavenward and whispered, "Your sister has done well, Parker. I know you've been looking out for her all these years. Hey, if you see Angela, tell her that I love and miss her."

Chapter 11

"So how are things going with Garland?" Jadin inquired when Ryker joined her and Jordin for lunch a few days later. They were celebrating Jadin's big win in court.

"Good," he responded. "The girls are bonding well."

"Are you and Garland bonding, as well?" Jordin asked while opening the menu. Her eyes traveled slowly over the selections.

"We're getting along, if that's what you mean. It helps that I have known her for a while. You remember Parker?"

Jadin and Jordin both nodded.

"Garland is his sister," Ryker announced.

Jadin gasped. "Are you serious?"

He gave a slight nod. "Yeah. It's a small world, isn't it?"

"That's for sure," Jadin responded.

"Maybe this will make the transition easier," Jordin interjected.

"Garland doesn't want the girls switched—she believes it would be too traumatic and confusing for them and I agree with her," he said. "She and I are trying to figure out what will work best for all of us."

"I would think she'd want to raise her own child." Jadin took a sip of her iced tea. "I know that I would if I were in her shoes."

"I'm not happy at the thought of giving up Kai," Ryker confessed. "She will always be my little girl. As far as I'm concerned, I now have two daughters."

"How does Garland feel?" Jadin questioned. "Does she feel the same way?"

"Yes, she does."

Jordin took a sip of her lemonade. "I can't wait to meet Amya."

Ryker grinned. "She looks just like Angela and she is absolutely adorable."

Jadin wiped her mouth on the edge of her napkin. "We now have two little angels to love on."

"I suppose this means that, in some way, Garland is now a member of our family," Jordin said.

He met Jordin's questioning gaze and nodded. "She is the mother of my children. She can never replace Angela's role completely, but Garland is the only mother Amya and Kai will ever know."

"Do you have feelings for Garland?" Jadin asked.

"She is Parker's little sister and she has been raising my daughter," Ryker responded. "Of course I care about her."

"I get the feeling that there's more going on between you."

"We know how much you loved Angela, but she's gone, Ryker," Jordin added. "She would not want you to be alone forever."

"I still feel married sometimes," he confessed.

Jadin pointed to his wedding ring. "Maybe it's because you're still wearing that."

"I guess it's time I took it off."

"You'll do it when you're ready," Jordin said.

"What are your plans for the weekend?" Jadin asked. "Are you in town or going to the beach?"

"We're all going to the beach Saturday. Kai is so excited."

Grinning, Jordin said, "I have a feeling that she's not the only one who's looking forward to tomorrow."

Ryker's expression remained neutral.

"The girls had a wonderful time today at the beach," Garland said as she eased a sleeping Amya into bed. Ryker watched from the doorway, then they headed down the hallway to the family room. "Why don't you let Kai stay here for tonight?"

"I…"

"You're more than welcome to sleep in the spare bedroom if you're not comfortable leaving her here with me, Ryker."

"Are you sure you don't mind?"

"I don't," she said. Truthfully, it bothered her some, but Garland understood his hesitancy. She was not ready to let Amya stay with him without her nearby.

"I just think it's too soon for a sleepover without me being present."

Garland smiled. "I understand. I appreciate you letting Kai spend the day with Amya and me. She called me Mommy today."

"Really?" He paused. "Well, I suppose it's natural. It's what she hears Amya call you."

She met his gaze. "Does it bother you that she calls me Mommy?"

Ryker shook his head. "You are her mother. Besides, Amya calls me Daddy. It's almost as if they know the truth somehow."

They settled down in the family room.

"What do you think about swimming lessons?" Garland asked. "For the girls."

"Aren't they a little too young?"

"No. Babies younger than them have taken swim classes," she explained. "I'll be there with them in the water."

Ryker nodded.

Not long after, Garland led him to the guest room, then headed to bed.

The room she had Ryker staying in featured a four-poster queen-size bed in mahogany, heaped with pillows in lacy cases and covered by a peach lace comforter. Ryker thought the room utterly feminine, but he'd only be sleeping there for one night.

Ryker went down the hallway to check on the girls before going into the bathroom to brush his teeth. He met Garland face to face outside of the guest bedroom.

"I was just coming to see if you needed anything before I checked on Kai and Amya."

He smiled. "I just looked in on them and they are fast asleep."

"Great," she murmured. "Do you need anything before I go to bed?"

Ryker shook his head. "No, I'm fine."

"Good night then," Garland stated. "I'll see you in the morning."

He gave a brief nod.

"Oh, and don't forget about the festival on Saturday. We're taking the girls."

"We will be there," Ryker promised. "I never knew that you were the one behind this annual event."

"It's the one thing I look forward to each year," she stated.

Garland smelled of lavender and roses.

Their eyes met and held.

Before Ryker realized what he was doing, he shifted closer, his hands in the silken curls, angling her head to increase the contact. When his lips touched hers, Garland let out a whimper that slayed him. For a heart-stopping moment he pushed aside the fact that she was Parker's little sister—that she was the sort of woman who would expect more than he could give.

She feathered her mouth across his in a way that was so soft that Ryker did not know what to do with the moment. The barely there touch of skin on skin managed to affect him more than a more carnal action could have. An odd, soft feeling seeped into his chest.

Garland suddenly stepped away from him.

He cleared his throat. "I have wanted to do that from the first moment I walked through your door."

"I guess we can put the kiss issue to rest then," she responded with a smile.

The smile on Garland's face left him wanting to kiss

her again. She was driving him wild with strange, complicated, confusing feelings.

"You are so beautiful," he murmured against her cheek.

"Good night, Ryker."

He had not intentionally remained celibate—in fact, he'd never imagined it was possible for him, but Angela's death had robbed him of many feelings. He also did not relish the idea of a string of women coming in and out of his daughter's life. Out of loyalty to both Angela and Kai, Ryker had not had sex even when his body protested.

Although he'd never acknowledged it before now, he was lonely. Ryker missed the benefits of sharing his life with someone special. At home, there were times he stayed awake or slept in one of the guest rooms at his home because he hated climbing into bed alone.

Sleep continued to elude him.

Ryker wished he could blame his restlessness on being in Garland's home, but he knew better. She had awakened his passion, his desire to be intimate, to love and to be loved.

Groaning, he rolled over to his left side, seeking slumber.

Garland could not wait to sink in the tub of bubbly water. It had been a long day and she was tired. She trailed her fingers in the hot liquid before sliding inside. She gasped at the water's loving embrace. After picking up the bar of soap that sat in a silver dish beside the tub, she bathed her body.

A few minutes later she got out and dried off with a

soft, fluffy towel. Garland picked up a bottle of scented body lotion and slathered it on her skin.

After dressing in a pair of pajama bottoms and a silk tank, she plumped up her pillows and sat up in bed. Garland would have trouble sleeping knowing that Ryker was just down the hall.

She placed her fingers to her mouth. *If he had kept his lips to himself, I wouldn't be in such a tizzy,* she thought. Garland had thought of him throughout the day, but he seemed oblivious to her beyond the fact that she was Kai's biological mother.

He acknowledged her and treated her with kindness, but never had she felt such longing for a man. Just talking to him had a raw hunger gnawing at her belly. When Ryker smiled, Garland felt it from the top of her head to the bottom of her feet and everywhere else in between.

None of the guys in her life compared to Ryker— no one could come close to the type of man that he had become. He was *that guy.* No other man would ever touch her heart the way Ryker had. She'd spent her college years fantasizing about him, but those fantasies had been futile.

He was not interested in her in that way. Yes, they'd shared a kiss or two, but Garland had no illusions about their relationship.

Chapter 12

Ryker heard Garland coming before he actually saw her. The hard tap of her high heels against the marble floor sounded out like tiny gunshots, even over the noise of the surrounding people. Garland never hesitated until she came to a halt in front of him. Her perfume reached for him, flavoring his every breath with the taste of her. He looked down into her eyes, saw them spark and flash and knew he was in deep trouble.

"You and Aubry did a great job with the anniversary party for your parents. This is really nice."

"I hope you're having a good time," he said.

"I am." She took a sip of her champagne. "How about you? Are you enjoying yourself?"

Ryker nodded. "I'm glad you're here, Garland."

She smiled. "I am, too."

Jadin and Jordin joined them.

"Garland, you look stunning," Jordin said. "Doesn't she, Ryker?"

"Yes," he responded with a grin.

"I'm going to check on the girls," Garland announced.

When she walked away, Jadin said, "I really like her. She's great with the girls. I can tell that she loves them both. If you're smart, you won't let her get away."

"My sister's right," Jordin interjected. "She's a keeper."

"Why don't you two worry about finding husbands instead of trying to find a wife for me?" Ryker suggested.

"Hey, don't worry about me," Jadin said. "I have a potential candidate. Jordin's the picky one."

"I know what I want," her sister said with a slight shrug.

"I'm going to find my date and the mother of my children." Ryker excused himself and went in search of Garland.

He found her upstairs in the room designated as a playroom for the girls. His mother also had had one of the bedrooms redecorated in a lavender-and-white theme for when Kai and Amya stayed over.

Garland was sitting in a rocking chair reading a story to the girls. Watching her, Ryker could see just how much she loved the girls. He loved them both just as much.

He kissed the girls good-night and went downstairs to his office.

Ryker sat at his desk, a Cheshire catlike grin dominating his face. He'd come up with the perfect solution. Instead of shuffling the girls back and forth between Edisto Island and Charleston, Garland and Amya could move in with him and Kai. This way they could raise the girls together.

It was perfect.

He could not wait to tell Garland. Ryker hoped that she would see that this was the best possible solution for the girls.

"I think I've come up with a solution. It's the best solution for everyone," he announced when Garland came downstairs.

"What is that?"

"You and Amya can move into my house," Ryker announced with a grin. "We can raise the girls together."

Her response was not what he was expecting.

"I'm not interested in being a nanny to the girls, Ryker," Garland stated coolly. "If this is what you have in mind…"

"Garland, I wasn't suggesting that at all," he said. "You are the mother of my girls. We will continue to coparent our daughters if you decide to stay on the island. But I really do believe that moving in here is the best possible solution for us. Don't you see? Neither one of us wants to give up the babies we raised, nor abandon our biological child."

"I just want to make things clear," she stated. "You really think living in the same house is the best option? My business is on Edisto Island. Amya attends school on the island. You want us to commute back and forth?"

"Do you have any other solution?" he asked. "Would you rather Kai and I move in with you?"

Garland thought for a moment. Her house was perfect for her and Amya, but she was sure Ryker wouldn't be happy there for long. It was probably more of a vacation-type home for him compared to this 4,500-square-foot house he currently lived in. "Not really."

"We get along fine, don't you think?"

She stirred uneasily in her chair. "Ryker, I'm not sure about this. If you don't mind, I'd like to take a few days just to think it over."

"That's fine. It's only a suggestion, Garland. If you have another idea, I want to hear it." Ryker doubted that she would be able to come up with another option. He knew that if she decided not to move to Charleston, then he and Kai would have to relocate to the island. He was willing to do whatever he could to keep his family together.

"Wow, this festival is really something," Ryker exclaimed. "The girls are going to have a ball."

"Good," Garland murmured. "My team and I have spent the past year preparing for this, so I want them to have a great time. We have more than a hundred creative and interactive activities, storytelling, arts and crafts, costumed characters and more."

He secured balloons for the girls, who squealed in delight.

"Bloon, Mommy," Amya shouted.

Kai pointed upward. "Look it, Mama."

Garland's eyes filled with tears. "She called me Mama."

Ryker gave her a tender smile. "Yes, she did."

Garland would have liked nothing more than to spend her day with them, but she had work to do. She divided her time between making sure everything was running as it should and checking on Ryker and the girls.

"Hey, why don't you take a minute and have lunch with us?" he suggested. "You've been all over the place, but I bet you haven't eaten anything. Sweetheart, you need to eat something."

Breathless, Garland checked her watch. "Sure, we can have lunch if you're ready to eat now." She looked closely at him.

Garland's heart skipped a beat at the worry she saw there. It had been a long time since anyone had been concerned over her. "I'm pacing myself, Ryker."

"This is a huge undertaking," he responded. "You did a great job. It's well put together."

"I've been doing it for four years now," she said as Ryker carried a tray of plates to a nearby table. Garland had Amya and Kai by the hand.

They made small talk while they ate.

"The girls are getting restless to see the puppet show," Ryker said. "I'd better take them over."

"I'll try to meet you there," Garland said. In the late July heat, her T-shirt clung to her, the hem on the sleeves heavy on her arms. Her shorts were not comfortable anymore, making her regret that she had not chosen to wear jeans.

The humidity during this part of the summer was not uncommon, but despite the temperature, people had come out in large numbers to attend the festival. Garland considered purchasing one of the sugary and slushy drinks that practically every child and teen had been buying all afternoon. She knew the festival would be ending soon, though.

Soon enough, three o'clock hit and the festival was over. Garland was exhausted but pleased with the success of the event. Ryker and the girls had left right after the puppet show. After taking care of housekeeping duties, she was soon on her way to his house.

The first thing Garland wanted to do was take a bath. Ryker met her at the door. "I know you're tired," he said, embracing her. "As soon as I heard you pull into the driveway, I started a bath for you. Take your time and I'll order dinner for us."

She gave him a grateful smile.

Ryker was such a sweetheart. He was very thoughtful, which was one of the qualities she loved about him.

Garland took her bath but never made it downstairs.

When Ryker came up to check on her, he found her lying in the middle of the bed, fast asleep.

The next morning, Ryker awoke to the delicious aroma of bacon frying. He quickly showered and dressed before going downstairs.

"Good morning," Garland greeted. "The girls are still sleeping. I'll get them up after I finish cooking breakfast. I hope you don't mind that I hijacked your kitchen."

"I don't mind at all. Need any help?"

She smiled at him. "No, thanks. I'm almost done."

"Kai loves pancakes."

"How does she feel about scrambled eggs?"

"She likes them with cheese."

Garland chuckled. "That's the way I eat them. When I was pregnant, I couldn't eat enough of them."

"She is definitely your daughter." Ryker stole a peek out of a nearby window. "The sun is shining," he observed. "It's a good day to visit the children's museum."

"Sounds good," Garland said. She turned off the stove after the last stack of pancakes was ready. "This should be more than enough for all of us."

Ryker picked up a strip of bacon and nibbled on it. "Being a parent seems to come natural to you."

Garland met his gaze. "Why do you say that?"

"I am always worried that I'm messing up with Kai.

I worry about how I'm going to explain girl stuff to her. You always seem at ease."

"Now you won't have to do it alone, Ryker," she told him. "Just so you know, parenting is an absorbed skill. I've made my share of mistakes, but I learn and move on."

"Good advice."

"Ryker, I'm sorry about falling asleep so early yesterday," Garland said. "I was so tired."

"It's fine. The girls and I watched a couple of Disney movies until they got sleepy."

"I've been thinking about your invitation to move in here."

"And?" Ryker prompted. "What did you decide?"

"I love my house and it's very comfortable, but there's not a lot of extra space to work with," Garland stated. "On the other hand, your house is huge but in Charleston."

"You don't want to commute..." he interjected.

"Actually, I don't mind the commuting," she told him. "After a lot of thought, I think Amya and I should move in with you and Kai. I really want to raise the girls together, and right now, I don't see any other solution."

He exhaled a long sigh of contentment. "You have no idea how much this means to me, Garland."

She smiled. "I think I do."

"This is the beginning of a new life for us."

Garland gloried briefly in the shared moment between them.

"Why are you in such a good mood?" Rochelle asked as she entered Ryker's office early Monday morning.

"Amya's coming home," he told her. "I asked Garland

to move into the house. Now the girls can really bond and go to the same school. It's a—"

"What are you thinking, Ryker? How could you move that woman into your house? You don't know her," Rochelle interjected.

His voice hardened ruthlessly. "That's where you're wrong. I do know Garland. I've known her for years."

"No, you knew her brother, Parker. You have no idea what type of woman she has become. Don't get me wrong—I'm glad Amya will be with you and Kai, but…"

"But nothing," he stated. "Garland is Amya and Kai's mother. I am not going to cut her out of their lives. It's wrong and you know it."

"I don't want you trapped by a woman who's all wrong for you, son." Her tone was coolly disapproving.

He shrugged off her words. "I'm a grown man. You seem to keep forgetting that."

"I haven't forgotten," Rochelle uttered. "You bring it up every chance that you get."

"I love you, Mom. I just do not like the way you keep interfering in my life." There was an edge to his voice. "You and Dad raised me well, so why can't you trust me to do right by my own children?"

"Son, I do trust you. It's Garland I'm not so sure about. Forgive me for being so protective of you and your sister, but there are so many manipulative people in the world."

"Aubry and I are intelligent people, Mom. We can take care of ourselves."

"I'm going to remind you of this situation a few years from now when the girls are older," Rochelle warned as she headed to the door. "I'm not happy with your decision, but it's your house and your life. I will tell you this, I won't stand by and let those girls get hurt, Ryker. Regardless of how you may feel about me."

Chapter 13

"I'm moving in with Ryker," Garland announced when she met with Trina. "We want to raise the girls together and we believe this is the best solution."

"Are you serious?" Trina asked. "You are actually going to move in with that man?"

She gave a slight nod. "It's the only way we can have what we want. I love both Amya and Kai. I don't want to give up either of them—neither does Ryker."

"So this is just a platonic kind of thing then?"

"Of course," Garland replied. "This is just about the girls."

Trina looked skeptical.

Garland folded her arms across her chest. "What exactly are you thinking right now?"

"I'm going to be honest with you because I love you. I'm not so sure this is a good idea. I don't want to see you get hurt."

She had not expected this response from her friend. "Trina, what do you suggest we do then?"

"Switch the girls, but continue to have a relationship with Ryker and his daughter."

"Trina, I am the only parent Amya has ever known," Garland argued. "I won't take that from her. The same goes for Ryker and Kai. Frankly, I'm surprised you would say that since you are her godmother. I thought you would understand why we want to raise them together."

"I love Amya and I will always be her godmother," Trina responded. "You asked my opinion and I gave it to you. But I'll support you in whatever you decide, Garland. You know that. I'm just worried you will get hurt."

"Why would I get hurt?"

"I know that you have feelings for Ryker."

"I have my emotions under control, Trina," Garland stated. "I don't have any illusions about Ryker. He is clearly very much in love with his late wife. He still wears his wedding ring."

"Oh."

"Yeah," she responded. "I'm not going to place myself in a position to get my heart broken."

"The girls are finally asleep," Garland announced. She and Amya had arrived behind the moving truck earlier in the day. Jordin had come over to entertain the girls while Ryker had helped Garland settle in.

Ryker handed her a cup of hot tea. "It feels perfect having them both here."

She nodded. "I hate to admit it, but you're right."

"I can help you with the rest of the unpacking," he offered.

Garland shook her head. "I can handle it."

A photo on the mantel over the fireplace caught her attention. It showed a much younger version of him with his arms slung around her and Parker. Garland smiled, remembering when they were college students and how much Ryker had made her laugh. It had been the most carefree time of her life.

"I wasn't really sure about this arrangement," Garland confessed. "I didn't know how or if we would get along under one roof."

"That's why we're going to take this one day at a time," he responded. "I'm sure we will have some disagreements, but I'm all for communication. We will just have to talk things out."

She took a sip of her tea. "Thanks for doing this, Ryker."

"I didn't just do it for the girls. I did it for us, as well."

Garland broke into a smile. "When we were in college, I always figured that you'd turn out to be some spoiled rich playboy. I'm glad that I was wrong."

"Did you really think that about me?"

She nodded. "I did, but you have turned into a great father. I'm sure you were a great husband, as well."

"I tried."

Garland thanked him for the tea, then went to her bedroom to finish the last of her unpacking. She was thankful that the day had ended. She had never liked moving. By the end of the night, Garland was exhausted, but all of her personal items were organized in the huge walk-in closet and dresser in her new bedroom. *My first apartment was the size of this closet,* she thought with a chuckle.

Ryker had not checked on her and she was fine with

that. He was a temptation she could not afford, so it was better if he didn't see her in such a weakened state.

Garland sat up, reached for the bottled water and took a long sip.

It seemed the entire DuGrandpre family showed up to welcome Garland and Amya to the family.

"Well, look who's coming up in the world," Trina said in a low whisper.

"Don't say things like that," Garland responded. "This is Ryker's home—not mine."

"I was kidding with you, but don't bother denying it. This is now your home, too."

"This house is huge," she whispered to Trina. "I've gotten lost twice already."

They laughed.

"Trina, there's a floor-to-ceiling library that's unbelievable. I have so many books, but they don't even come close to filling up that room. Ryker's books are mostly law related so he has them in his office. The girls even have bookshelves stuffed with reading material in their playroom."

"I can't wait to see it."

"In a little while I'll give you the grand tour."

"Go see to your other guests. I'm going to sit over there with your mother."

Just then Ryker's aunt and uncle arrived and he gestured for Garland to join him. "I want to introduce you to my uncle Etienne DuGrandpre and my aunt Patricia."

"It's very nice to meet you, dear," Patricia DuGrandpre said. Her husband was a lot more reserved, though he gave her a brief hug.

While they waited for Aubry to serve the food, Ryker and Garland continued to tend to their guests.

Garland noted that a bit of tension accompanied the conversations going on through the room. And she could sense Rochelle's eyes following her every movement. But she did her best to brush off any negativity.

Forty-five minutes later, everyone was seated at tables around the pool. Garland deliberately sat far from Rochelle. She had no idea why the woman did not like her, but she'd decided not to let her ruin her day.

After dinner, Garland and her mother excused themselves to grab slices of apple pie from the buffet in the kitchen. Ryker had warned her that his sister's homemade flaky crust and spicy apples were not only delicious but also addictive. The dessert was still warm and she could not wait to sample it.

In one corner of the family room, she and Elaine could see Amya and Kai squeal happily as they played together. Jordin then turned on some music and began dancing. The girls joined her before collapsing into laughter when Ryker, who'd just come in, decided to show off his moves.

"They are both darling," Elaine whispered as she picked up a plastic bowl. "And very happy."

Garland handed her the serving spoon. "They get along so well. They've bonded as sisters."

"Kai looks just like you did when you were her age."

"Mama, I'm so glad that you're here with us."

"Me, too."

They sat down at the kitchen table to eat.

"This is so delicious," her mother said. "Ryker's sister made it?"

Garland nodded. "She has her own restaurant. Remember, I told you about that."

"I think you did mention it." Her mother glanced across the room. "Who is that lady staring at Amya? Is she the nanny?"

"We don't have a nanny, Mama. That woman is Amya's grandmother. She's Angela's mother."

"I don't like the way she and her husband are looking at Amya."

"It's fine, Mama," Garland assured her. "This is the first time they are meeting her."

"I'm going to sit over there in case they try to snatch my baby. I'm not letting that happen."

"None of the DuGrandpres will let her take Amya or Kai."

"I hope you're right. Anyway, you look so happy, hon. I'm so glad you and Ryker found each other."

Garland smiled. "I am very happy, Mama." She really was content, she realized with astonishment. Garland *liked* being here with Ryker and she was amazingly comfortable with him.

Feeling at home was foreign to Garland. Because she'd been a foster child, she had never really felt she had a home, even with Parker. She knew his mother loved her like her own daughter, but the truth was that she was not Elaine's daughter.

As if her mother could read her thoughts, she said, "I'm sorry, Garland. I should have adopted you like your dad and I planned. I want you to know that I don't need any papers—you are my darling daughter. I love you more than my own life."

She reached over and took Elaine's hand. "I know that, Mama. I love you, too."

"Speaking of mothers, that Rochelle DuGrandpre is still as uppity as she's always been," Elaine uttered.

Garland stole a peek over her shoulder before saying, "She's okay. I just don't let her get to me."

"Good."

At that moment Garland felt a migraine coming on and excused herself to escape upstairs.

"I see you've settled right in," Rochelle said, stepping out into the hallway.

"Are you following me?" Garland questioned, trying to keep the irritation out of her voice. "I just came up here to have five minutes of quiet."

"Are you tired of us already?"

"No, that's not it at all," she responded. "I have a headache and I came up here to grab some medicine and wait for it to kick in."

What she did not need right now was Rochelle Du-Grandpre tracking her every move.

"Did you need something?" she asked.

"This is my son's house," Rochelle stated coolly. "If I need anything, I'll just let him know."

Garland waved her hand in resignation. "If Ryker starts looking for me, will you please let him know that I'll be down in a few minutes?"

"Sure. I'm going to go join the other guests downstairs."

She did not care where the woman went as long as she was far away from her.

Garland's head was beginning to throb with pain.

She lay down across her bed and closed her eyes.

Chapter 14

Ryker was pleased that everyone seemed to be having a good time. But then his gaze strayed to his mother-in-law, who was walking toward him and looked like she had a bad taste in her mouth.

"She looks just like my Angela. She and Kai get along so well."

"They are siblings," Ryker said firmly. "Garland and I intend to raise them together as such."

"How could you just let this woman move in here?" Edna Harvey demanded. "This house was Angela's home. Have you forgotten my daughter already?"

"It's also *my* house," Ryker stated, spacing the words evenly. "I will never forget Angela. She will always be in my heart."

Stiffening she muttered, "I am well aware of this. It's just that you and Angela lived in this house as husband

and wife. Now you have some other woman living here. It bothers me."

"I'm sorry you feel that way. As for Garland, she hasn't done anything wrong," Ryker stated. "She is as much a victim in this as I am. I am not going to allow you to be rude to her. She wants the best for both girls and so do I."

"I see my opinion doesn't matter."

"It doesn't," he confirmed. "I'm not trying to be rude, but I know what's right for my daughters. Now if you will excuse me, I need to see to the rest of my guests. Feel free to stay around, but I'll understand if you and Dad would prefer to leave."

Ryker released a short sigh of relief as he walked briskly away from Edna.

"Hey, I was just looking for you," Ryker said.

"I was upstairs," Garland responded. "I felt a migraine coming on and needed to take some medication."

"Are you feeling better?"

"I am," she confirmed. "Where are the girls?"

"Jordin and Jadin took them upstairs to get ready for bed."

"They should be enjoying the party. I'll relieve them."

Ryker stopped her. "They want to do it. Jordin gave me strict orders to make sure *you* enjoy the party."

"Can we at least check on them?" she asked.

He nodded.

They walked toward the girl's bedroom just as the twins were coming out. Jadin made shooing motions.

"They're just about to fall asleep," Jordin said in a low voice.

"I guess it's time we returned to our guests," Ryker

told Garland. "My uncle and aunt are just about to leave."

"Let's go say our good-byes then," she said, pasting on a smile.

Garland would have preferred to stay upstairs with her children than venture back down into hostile territory. She felt a shred of guilt over the thought. Everyone had been nice to her—all except for Rochelle DuGrandpre. She thought that Garland was after their money.

She does not know me at all. Garland valued love and honesty above all else. Material items came and went, just like some family members, as far as she was concerned.

Downstairs, she continued to avoid Ryker's mother. And Garland even managed to enjoy the rest of her evening.

The last guest left shortly before midnight.

"I don't think your mother likes me very much," Garland stated as she sat down on the sofa beside Ryker.

"It's not that she doesn't like you—she doesn't know you yet. My mother doesn't warm up to people easily. It's because of the way she grew up."

"I hope that she knows that I don't want any of your money. I just want to get to know my daughter."

"We both want the same thing," Ryker stated. "I've told my mother that."

"I can see that you're very close to your family."

He nodded. "Yeah…I am."

"I think it's great," Garland murmured. "I'm so glad my mom was able to come tonight. In addition to depression, she also suffers from fibromyalgia, so she's not always able to get out and about."

"I'm sorry to hear that," Ryker responded. "How does she feel about you living here with me?"

"She's okay with it. Actually, Mama thinks it's great because it's you."

"Yeah?"

Nodding, Garland smiled. "She has always loved you like a son, Ryker. She has been so depressed lately, so I wasn't sure if she was going to come to the party, but I'm glad she did. I think it does her good to get out every now and then."

Ryker was not a man of impulse, but he yearned to pull Garland into his arms and kiss her passionately. He struggled to remain a chivalrous yet wretched gentleman.

Instead, he thanked her for her help at the party and they both headed to their separate rooms. He thought about going to her room but changed his mind after his eyes traveled over to Angela's photograph on the nightstand.

Ryker jumped in the shower. He had no idea just how long he stood under the hot spray of water.

He dried off with a fluffy towel, his thoughts on the woman sleeping in his guest room. While Garland slept peacefully, Ryker was anything but sleepy. He lay in bed for almost an hour picturing Garland in various stages of undress.

Frustrated, Ryker slipped on a pair of pajama pants and slippers. *A piece of apple pie sounds good right now,* he thought as he proceeded downstairs. *Might as well have some ice cream, too.* Anything to take his mind off Garland.

Garland strolled out of her bedroom clad in silk pajama bottoms and a lace-trimmed camisole. She did not expect to find Ryker in the family room watching television with an empty plate in front of him.

"I didn't know you were down here," she said, her eyes glued to his bare muscled chest.

"I came down for my sister's apple pie. I thought you were sleeping," he told her.

"No, I'm in the mood for ice cream."

He glanced up at her. "No pie?"

"I had some earlier that I'll have to work off the rest of the week," she responded with a grin. "Come to think of it, I really don't need to eat ice cream, either."

"Want to watch a movie instead?" he asked her. "No calories."

She nodded. "Sure." Garland sat down on the sofa. "What's coming on?"

Ryker handed her the remote. "You have a choice of action and adventure, comedy, romance or horror."

"How about action?" Garland asked.

"Really?"

"Why are you surprised? I love action movies. I used to go to the movies with you and Parker, remember?"

"Oh yeah…that's right."

"You probably don't remember because you always had some girl wrapped around you."

He laughed. "You're not so innocent yourself. I remember a boy or two stealing kisses from you when you didn't think we were paying attention."

"I don't know what you're talking about Ryker."

"Yeah, you do."

Garland's smile was fond. "We had some good times back then."

"We did," he agreed.

"I really wish that the girls could've met Parker. He loved kids and he would have been the best uncle ever."

"He would have been a great uncle," Ryker agreed.

"You're a great father, Ryker. I want you to know that."

"Thank you," he responded. "I have tried my best. My dad is not a demonstrative man, but my sister and I know he loves us. Sometimes, I think Aubry feels otherwise. He was always so busy and he had no interest in the things that she liked when we were growing up. Don't get me wrong, though, he tried to be there for her. But even though he was present, it was like he really wasn't. I don't want my daughters to feel that way about me."

"You won't have to worry about that," Garland assured him. "Amya and Kai both adore you."

"I watch them while they sleep," Ryker confessed. "I want to see if Amya's a quiet sleeper or if she burrows under the covers like Kai."

"I love the way Kai murmurs under her breath whenever she's concentrating on something. You can tell that she's really trying to figure out whatever it is."

Ryker broke into a grin. "I'm glad you agreed to move in."

"Do you think we're able to be together like this most of the time without changing anything?"

"I guess we should discuss the elephant in the room."

"When you initially proposed the idea of us living together and raising the girls, you made it sound like a corporate merger."

"Was I that impersonal?"

Garland nodded. "I didn't expect you to pretend to be in love with me, but it would've been nicer if it was more because you liked me."

Ryker reached over and took her hand in his own. "You know that I like you. I like you a lot, Garland. Since we're talking about this, I might as well admit that I'm still very attracted to you."

Her soft exhalation sounded as if a tremor passed through her. Garland looked fiercely at him. "We're attracted to each other."

"I've been thinking about the picture we're painting for our daughters," Ryker stated.

"What about it?"

"We're living here together but we're not married."

Garland chuckled. "We're not sleeping together, Ryker. It's innocent."

"We know this, but this is not how the rest of the world will view it."

"You're really serious about this, aren't you?" she asked. "The girls are two years old. They don't know anything about relationships."

"Garland, what do you think about marriage?"

"How did we get to this subject?"

"I think we should get married."

She gasped. "You can't be serious."

"I am very serious, Garland. It would make us a real family."

"But…marriage." She had not considered the possibility, especially because Ryker was still grieving the loss of his wife.

"We're friends and we get along well," he was saying. "We want the best for our daughters and if anything ever happened to me—you and the girls would be well taken care of."

"Ryker, you're not ready for marriage."

"Angela is gone and she will never come back. That part of my life is over, Garland."

"I have always dreamed of marrying a man who loves me."

"You don't think we can learn to love each other?"

"I can't believe we're having this discussion right now. It must be because it's late and we're tired."

Ryker shook his head. "That's not it at all."

"Why don't we table this discussion for a couple of days?" Garland suggested. "I can't rush into something I believe is sacred."

"I understand," he told her.

She rose to her feet. "Good night, Ryker."

He grabbed her by the arms and kissed her mindlessly, molding their bodies together. Garland could very easily give into her needs—needs that were screaming in desire, but it wasn't the best choice for her to make.

She had never expected Ryker to bring up the subject of marriage. Garland cared for him, but a marriage in name only—she was not sure this was the route to take. Neither one of them wanted to lose the girls… She released a long sigh.

Garland was a romantic at heart. She wanted love, romance, all of it. The reality was that they had two little girls depending on them. Having parents who were married would provide a better sense of security.

Sometime around dawn, she managed to drift off into a less than restful slumber.

Marriage was for a lifetime.

At least Ryker intended it to be, and it was not something he glibly approached. He had given this a lot of thought.

He'd married Angela for love, although their happily-ever-after was not as long as he had hoped. This time around, Ryker wanted to marry someone he cherished and honored and with whom he could build a family.

Suddenly Garland was standing right in front of him, bringing her scent and the clear skin of her beautiful face close to his. He leaned back and looked down at her. "Good morning."

"Good morning," she responded with a bright smile. Ryker elected to ignore the twitch of her luscious lips. Instead, he placed a kiss on her cheek.

"Want anything special for breakfast?" Garland asked.

"What would you say if I said that I wanted you?"

Her eyes closed briefly, and when she met his gaze again, she replied, "It's not nice to be such a tease. If you don't tell me what you want to eat, I'll just throw something together."

He laughed. "How about a ham and cheese omelet then?"

"Sounds good to me."

"You know how to make an omelet?" Ryker asked, surprised.

"I am a very good cook," Garland responded. "And yes, I can make an omelet. I guess you forgot I used to work in a diner."

He had forgotten. "That's right."

"I think the girls are up, so why don't you bring them down for breakfast?" Garland suggested. "I'll make them cheese eggs."

"We'll be back down in a few," he said.

He paused a moment to watch her. She was so focused on preparing the ingredients for the omelets that she hadn't noticed he was still in the kitchen. The pull of Garland was inexorable and something Ryker was tired of fighting.

Chapter 15

"I've given our talk a lot of thought," Garland stated as she entered Ryker's office a couple of days later. He had been home for about an hour, and she had wanted to give him some time to relax before announcing her decision.

Garland had thought long and hard about marrying Ryker. She was willing to do anything for the sake of her daughters, including marrying a man she knew did not love her.

He looked up from his computer screen. "What did you decide?"

"You were talking about a marriage in name only, right?" She needed to be sure they were on the same page.

"Initially, but I'm open to loving again."

"You really want to do this?"

Ryker nodded.

"You do know that your family is going to go ballistic," she said with a tiny smile.

"You and the girls are my family, so what do you say? Will you marry me?"

"I can't believe I'm saying this, but yes. I'll marry you, Ryker."

He reached into his pocket but Garland stopped him by saying, "I hope you don't have a ring for me."

"You don't want a ring?"

"I want a ring when you decide that I am the woman for you and what's between us is forever."

"You don't want to even see it?" he asked.

"No."

Ryker dropped his hand to his side. "Okay, so how much time do you need to plan a wedding?"

"None," Garland responded. "We can have a minister come here to the house or we can go to the justice of the peace."

"You don't want a wedding?"

"Ryker, it's not like this is going to be a real marriage."

"We may be taking a different route but the marriage will be a real one. We are going to take our time getting to know each other as husband and wife. I want our wedding day to be special—one that you will always cherish. I want you to wear my ring, Garland."

"I will agree to a very simple wedding band."

"You are very stubborn, but I'll do this your way," he said with a sigh. "We can apply for a license today."

"Okay," she said quietly.

"I promise that you won't regret this, Garland. I won't do anything to hurt you or the girls."

"You'd better not," she warned. "You do remember that I am a fifth-degree black belt."

"Actually, I'd forgotten all about that," Ryker laughed. "You and Parker used to attend competitions."

"Seems like a lifetime ago," she murmured. "Parker and I had this dream of teaching tae kwon do to disadvantaged youth... I guess that dream died with him."

"It's not too late, sweetheart. Do it for the kids and for Parker."

Garland met his gaze. "Maybe I will...one day."

"We can find you space in Charleston to conduct your classes. Maybe I'll even sign up for a class. With Amya and Kai. See, you already have three students."

His words sparked a smile from her. "I just might do it," she said. "Thanks for the gentle push, Ryker."

They spent the rest of the evening planning their wedding. For the most part, Ryker was taking care of everything. Somewhere deep inside, Garland wanted this marriage to be a real one. They had great chemistry. But it could easily evaporate after the wedding, she thought. She forced herself to be more optimistic.

Wouldn't it be so much better if they fell in love? Then they could be a real family.

Four days later, on Saturday, their wedding day dawned bright and sunny. Her pastor was scheduled to arrive in four hours and then their ceremony would begin.

Garland's stomach was churning and she was shivering uncontrollably. Wedding jitters? She had no idea. Her breathing came out in short pants.

On hearing of the wedding, Ryker's family had displayed mixed emotions. His twin cousins were delighted; his sister voiced her reservations about the marriage but vowed to support the decision because of the girls. His mother was displeased and made sure everyone knew it. His father decided to simply congratulate them and leave it at that. Her mother's shock was evident, but she thought it a good idea. Angela's parents were worried that he was moving much too soon and would forget all about his late wife.

Garland fingered the simple ivory gown that would serve as her wedding dress. She would soon be Mrs. Ryker DuGrandpre. It was a dream come true for her... almost.

He was not in love with her.

Her feelings for Ryker were strong, but she also could not classify them as love. But Garland knew that loving him would come easy for her, though she would be mindful to keep her heart guarded.

A knock on her door ripped Garland out of her reverie. "Ryker, you can't come in."

"It's me."

She rushed to the door, opening it just enough to let in her visitor. "Mama, when did you get here?"

"Just a few minutes ago," she responded. "Everything downstairs looks beautiful, sweetie. This is a really gorgeous house."

"Did you see Ryker?"

She nodded. "He's down there barking orders to everyone. He wants everything perfect for you."

Garland smiled. "It's really sweet, but I told him that we didn't need to have a wedding. I wanted to go to the justice of the peace—just the two of us—but Ryker wasn't having it."

"I'm glad he did it this way. You've always wanted a wedding."

"I wanted one where everyone would be happy for the bride and groom. Ryker's mom is anything but happy about this union."

"Hon, enjoy your special day, regardless of that woman."

"I need to check on the girls," Garland responded as she opened the door.

Jordin was in the hallway. "Ryker can't see you before the wedding. Stay in your room. I'll bring the girls to you after I get dressed."

"Thank you for everything, Jordin."

She hugged her. "You're good for my cousin. My sister and I could see it. And soon the rest of the family will see it, too. Don't let Aunt Rochelle get to you. This is *your* day."

"Same thing I just told her," her mother interjected.

Jordin embraced her. "Welcome to the family, cousin."

"Thank you."

"I'm going to get the little ladies ready," she said. "See you in a few."

Garland was close to tears. She needed and wanted a family so much. Now she would have that, albeit in name only. This was a start, something for her to hold on to.

A few minutes later her eyes filled with tears at the sight of Amya and Kai in matching kiwi-colored dresses with frothy, full skirts and flowers in their hair.

"Jordin, they look so adorable. Thank you."

"Mommy, gimme kiss," Amya said.

"I want kiss, too," Kai stated.

"C'mere, my babies," Garland told them. "I have

enough kisses to go around." She hugged and kissed them both.

"Okay, Mommy has to get ready for her wedding," Jordin announced. "She's marrying Daddy today. Yay!"

"Yay!" the girls repeated in unison.

Garland laughed. "They have no idea what is going on."

Jordin checked her phone. "Jadin just texted to say that she's on her way up to help you get dressed. I'm going to take the girls downstairs."

"Thanks again for all of your help and the dresses. They really are gorgeous."

"You have to thank Robyn for the dresses," Jordin confessed. "She found them and had them shipped in time for the wedding."

"She is so wonderful. I've been thinking about making her the manager of the boutique so that I can spend more time with Ryker and the girls."

"I think it's a great idea."

It was time for Garland to get dressed. The twins had taken her to a spa the day before for a complete make-over from head to toe. When she looked at her reflection in the full-length mirror, Garland barely recognized her reflection.

She turned around slowly in a circle to see herself. The dress was simple but perfect for the ceremony.

The hour soon arrived for Garland to make her entrance. Her mother escorted her down the stairs and into the living room, where family members had gathered. Her breath caught in her throat as she saw Ryker standing near the pastor. He was stunning in a classic tailor-made suit with a crisp white shirt.

Jordin and Jadin were grinning at her as she slowly

made her way down the aisle. Garland deliberately avoided looking at Rochelle DuGrandpre because she wanted the ceremony to begin on a bright note.

Her pastor began by saying, "Dearly beloved…"

Garland stole a glance at Ryker and smiled.

He returned her smile as they listened to Pastor Holly talk about the sanctity of marriage for better or worse. She heard every word he said and wondered what was going through Ryker's head in that moment. Garland knew he'd probably never expected to hear those words again as a groom.

Will he ever love me? she wondered as her eyes connected with Ryker's gaze.

It took everything in Ryker not to run up and hug Garland. He turned his head a fraction to look at his daughters. They were so radiant and all grins. His heart flipped at seeing the toddlers holding hands. They were sisters.

"Do you, Garland Ashton Warner, take this man, Ryker Jacques DuGrandpre…" Pastor Holly began.

"I do," she said, repeating the vows that meant forever while gazing into his eyes.

"Do you, Ryker Jacques DuGrandpre, take this woman, Garland Ashton Warner…"

"I do," he responded in a strong, confident voice.

When they were pronounced husband and wife, everyone applauded except for his mother. If Angela's parents had chosen to attend the wedding they likely would not have clapped, either. Ryker was disappointed they hadn't come, but he knew that Garland most likely felt relief at their absence.

They were married. Garland was his wife.

The newlyweds celebrated with a catered dinner in

lieu of a grand reception, much to his mother's dismay. She'd wanted them to have a huge formal dinner to announce Ryker's marriage, but Garland had balked at the idea.

Rochelle was controlling and a force to be reckoned with, but he admired Garland for refusing to let his mother intimidate her.

"Your bride certainly looks happy," Rochelle stated in a low whisper, cornering her son. "She should be, since she's won what is equivalent to the lottery."

Ryker sent her a sharp look. "Mom, don't start."

"What are you thinking, son? No prenup?"

"There was no prenup when I married Angela, either," Ryker pointed out. "I've told you before that Garland is not interested in our family's money. Her business is doing quite well."

Rochelle sighed in resignation. "I guess you'll have to learn the hard way."

"Let's not do this today, Mom. It's my wedding day."

"Fine. Can I take the girls home with me tonight?" she asked. "You should spend your wedding night alone with your bride, even if it's not a real marriage." The expression on his face prompted her to add, "I didn't mean that the way it sounded, Ryker."

"I'll check with Garland and let you know," he told her.

He found his new wife sitting on the sofa with Trina. He smiled and joined them. "My mother would like to have the girls spend the night with her and Dad, so we can spend our wedding night alone."

She gazed at him. "Is this what you want to do?"

"Sure," Ryker responded. "Do you have a problem with it?"

"Of course you two should be alone on your wedding night," Trina quickly interjected.

Garland wanted to protest, but she would only be doing so to place a barricade between herself and her new husband. Instead, she said, "Your mom may not like me, but I know she loves Amya and Kai. It's fine."

As Garland's mother approached, Ryker stood and said, "I can't tell you how happy I am to see you, Mrs. Moscot."

"I had to be here for my little girl. You know you don't have to be so formal with me. You used to call me Mom Elaine."

He embraced her. "I have really missed you and I'm sorry I didn't come around much after…"

She nodded in understanding. "I know. No apologies needed."

"Well, I guess I'll be seeing you more now that I'm your son-in-law," he said with a smile. Then he turned to Garland. "I guess we should make our rounds once more before saying good-night to everyone."

Trina laughed. "I think we're about to be kicked out."

Elaine nodded and smiled.

"I would like to spend some quality time with my bride," Ryker confessed.

Garland looked surprised for a moment but recovered quickly. She walked over to her mother-in-law and said, "Thank you for offering to keep the girls tonight. Ryker and I really appreciate it."

"You're quite welcome." Her tone had its normal chill to it.

"I know that you don't agree with our decision to marry, but it was nice having you attend the wedding. It wouldn't have been the same without you."

"The ceremony was sweet," Rochelle uttered. "However, I don't want to see my granddaughters get hurt when your *marriage* to my son falls apart."

"Enjoy this time with your grandbabies, Mrs. Du-Grandpre," Garland responded before walking away. She was trying her best to get along with this woman, but Rochelle was not making it an easy task.

After everyone had gone, Ryker joined her in the family room.

Garland was watching a movie on Lifetime. He sat down beside her on the plush sofa, sinking into its comfort.

She turned off the television. It was their wedding night, after all. *What does he have in mind?* Garland wondered.

"I'm glad your mother understood our decision to get married," he said as he settled back against the cushions.

Garland heaved a sigh of relief. She could make conversation. "It seemed like the perfect solution to her, as well."

"I hope that I didn't rush you into something you didn't really want."

She met his gaze. "We did rush into this marriage, but it makes sense."

"My father used to tell me that logic and emotions don't always take the same route. I wanted to get married again one day. I wanted Kai to have a mother. Now that I have Amya and you, I'm a happy man," Ryker stated. "Arranged marriages have worked, you know. I believe that if we work together, we can make this one work."

Garland became silent.

"What's that look for?" he questioned.

"Making our marriage work lacks emotion and passion. I know that we're not in love, but I really don't want this to be a business merger—more of a friendship. I can deal with that label."

"You must know that I care for you, Garland." Ryker held out a hand to her. "You are my wife now. I don't take that for granted because marriage means something to me."

She placed her hand in his and felt his fingers tighten. Garland silently acknowledged that it would not be hard to love Ryker. The determination to make their marriage a real one and his caring reminded her of the man she'd crushed on all those years ago.

They sat with their hands intertwined. Garland's heart seemed to pound so hard that it was audible. She gazed over at Ryker, noticing a glint in his eyes that warmed her from head to toe.

"You're welcome to make any changes to the house," he stated after a moment. "This is your home, too."

"Thank you, but everything is so beautiful already. Though I would like to add some of my artwork and sculptures throughout."

"Have at it," Ryker said. "We can start from scratch if you want."

Garland could not remember how long it had been since she had felt anything like this. She had dreamed of being with Ryker but simply figured he was out of her league.

She sat there chewing on her bottom lip.

"I know that we said this marriage would start off in name only, but I expect that to change at some point," Ryker stated. "I won't rush you, Garland. We will consummate our marriage when you're ready."

"Thank you," she murmured. "It's been a long day. I

don't know about you, but I'm tired," Garland said with what she hoped was an apologetic smile. "I think I'm going to bed."

He kissed her gently on the lips. "Thank you for agreeing to be my wife."

"I'm glad we did it."

Ryker smiled. "Good night, Garland. Sleep well."

She ascended the stairs to the second level, new hope for her family bubbling in her chest.

Chapter 16

Ryker knew he was not alone in hoping that he and Garland would find love. He was not alone in wanting to love. He wanted to believe that they would find it together. He looked forward to coming home to delicious scents of dinner cooking, the laughter of children and relaxing evenings with his wife.

With Garland.

This would be a nice change of pace for Ryker. Life just seemed so much easier when he was married.

Except tonight.

Tonight was his wedding night and he was alone in his king-size bed. Deep down, Ryker had hoped Garland would want to move into the master bedroom. He had hoped that she had some passionate feelings about him.

Ryker intended to keep his word about not rushing her to make love. But he could not ignore the yearning within or the guilt he felt for wanting her.

Angela was gone, but he still felt as though he was betraying her somehow.

He reminded himself that he could not allow his emotions to take over. Ryker did not want to hurt Garland in any way. They were taking their marriage one day at a time.

They had been married a couple of weeks and things were good between them concerning the girls. And Ryker was careful to stay within the boundaries he had set for their marriage, Garland acknowledged.

It was a struggle for her to be in the same room with Ryker. He had always been *that guy* for her. However, he had also been off-limits. Now they were married, but it was not exactly a dream come true for Garland.

From where she was in the kitchen, she could hear the garage doors going up. Ryker was home.

"Traffic was crazy, but I made it home," he announced, coming through the side entrance from the garage.

Garland turned from the oven with a welcoming smile. "Girls," she called, "your daddy's home."

The seconds ticked by as they stared at each other.

Ryker made a move toward her, planting a kiss on her cheek.

Little feet thundered down the hallway and Ryker found himself surrounded by two little giggling girls.

Garland stepped out of the way so that the girls could properly greet their father. Their eyes connected once more before Ryker picked the girls up one by one, planting kisses on each of them.

A few minutes later, Amya and Kai disappeared

as quickly as they had come, leaving him alone with Garland.

He went toward Garland, who was stirring something on the counter. "What's that?" he asked.

"I'm making cornbread to go with the roast chicken and collard greens."

"Everything smells good."

"We can eat as soon as the bread is ready," she said.

Ryker wanted to kiss her nape in the worst way. What if he just went over and kissed her passionately? They were married after all.

Celibacy had been no more than an occasional irritation until now. He was very aware of Garland in the house.

She was bustling around Ryker as if he were not even there. If he had been eyeing her lustfully, he was sure that Garland had not noticed.

Despite his hunger for her, Ryker was thrilled to come home and find dinner cooking. It was also nice that the girls had been able to stay home with Garland today instead of going to school.

The truth was that he was glad not to be alone anymore—that it no longer was just him and Kai.

At the dinner table, Garland said grace.

"Are you okay?" he inquired after she remained quiet afterward.

She met his gaze. "Yeah, why do you ask?"

"You seemed troubled or something."

"They're too young to know what's happened," Garland murmured. "How do we explain this stuff to them when they're older?"

"I don't know," he admitted. "But I'm sure we'll figure out something when that time comes."

"I guess you're right."

"Oh, I didn't tell you?" Ryker asked, his face serious. "I'm always right."

Garland burst into laughter.

He grinned devilishly. "Why are you laughing? I'm serious."

As they finished dinner, he announced, "Angela's father called. They want to see the girls."

She met his gaze. "You mean they want to see Amya."

"Her grandparents want to meet her, but they also want to see Kai."

"When?"

"They would like to come on Saturday," Ryker responded. "Will you be home?"

"Yes," Garland responded. "I want to meet them, as well." She hoped they would not react like Rochelle. It was going to be awkward, she knew. After all, Ryker had married their daughter and fathered their grandchild. Surely, they did not begrudge him any happiness.

The thought lingered on her mind. They did not have a real marriage and she needed to remember that.

Ryker continued to experience emotions that had not surfaced since his wife's death. In fact, his feelings for Garland were deepening. But he held on to his feelings for Angela, afraid that if he let go of them, memories of their life together would fade. And she deserved better than that.

Ryker knew that it was not Angela's choice to leave him. He also knew that he had to continue life without her. The last time he had visited her grave was the night before his wedding to Garland. He wanted her to know that his visits would continue and that he would make sure their daughter knew the woman who'd given her life loved her deeply.

"You must be thinking about Angela," Garland said as she sat down beside Ryker. "Do you want to talk about her?"

"I'm not ready."

Garland nodded in understanding.

"After Parker died, there were so many times I wanted to call you," Ryker blurted out.

"Then why didn't you?"

"I guess I didn't really know what I'd say to you, Garland. I knew how close you two were and when he died...seeing you and your mother at the funeral was hard." He sighed in resignation. "I'm sorry that I wasn't there for you."

"I survived," she responded with a slight shrug. "Besides you had your own life, Ryker. You were in law school and you were seeing Angela. It's not like we were that close or anything."

"Garland, I cared for you—a lot, but I didn't want to cross boundaries. The truth is that I knew if I'd reached out, those lines would have been crossed."

"That's quite an assumption," she responded.

"Are you telling me that you never felt anything for me?" Ryker challenged. "Because I know different."

She knew that he was talking about the passionate kiss they'd shared in college. "That was a long time ago, Ryker."

"We almost ended up in bed that night, Garland. Are you saying that you feel absolutely nothing for me now?"

She had feelings for Ryker. Deep feelings, but she was not sure she was ready to tell him so. "I do care for you as a friend."

He burst into laughter.

Garland decided to be honest with him. Apparently, she was not as good at hiding her feelings as she thought. "Okay, I'm attracted to you, Ryker. There, I've said it."

"That was like pulling teeth."

"It was not," she argued. "It's just not something we need to be focusing on at the moment, especially because of Angela."

Ryker frowned in confusion. "What does she have to do with this?"

"You still love her, Ryker," Garland stated. "Her death has been very hard on you and I'm not blind. I can tell that you're still grieving."

"I will always love Angela, but it's been time for me to move on for a while. I'm finally ready to do that."

She reached over and took his hand in her own. "Ryker, you're not ready, but it's okay. Don't try to force something. We're good."

Garland swallowed her sadness. She could not let him know how much it pained her to love a man who was still in love with someone else.

"I know you, Garland," Ryker told her. "You never would've married me if you did not have strong feelings for me."

Their gaze met and held, making Garland nervous. She thought she detected a flicker in his intense eyes, causing her pulse to skitter alarmingly.

"I know that you believe I am unable to move on without Angela, but you're wrong. I don't want to discuss her anymore—I would rather focus on you and me."

"What about us?"

"You are as attracted to me as I am to you," Ryker responded. "It's been that way since college, but I never acted on that attraction back then because of Parker."

Garland did not respond.

"Am I wrong about your feelings for me?"

"No," she responded. "I had a huge college girl's crush on you." She glanced over at him. "Why are we talking about this now?"

"Because I'm still very attracted to you."

"I'm not quite sure how to respond to that," she said.

"You are so beautiful," he said.

"What are you doing, Ryker?"

"I'm being honest with you, Garland. It's what we agreed to do."

"Okay, you're attracted to me. Now what? You do know that I'm not that same girl I was in college, right? I'm not going to swoon in a puddle at your feet like those girls did when we were in school."

He laughed. "Understood."

"Ryker, I…I am attracted to you, but my focus is making sure the girls are thriving."

"We have to have a life outside of the children, Garland," he stated. "Since you've been here, I'm realizing it more and more."

"I'm thinking what you're feeling is lust, Ryker. Let's not get it confused."

He laughed. "I can always count on you to be straight up with me."

"I don't know any other way to be," she responded.

"I'm not complaining. I like that about you." He paused. "Let's have dinner out tomorrow night. It will be a date night."

"Date night?" she repeated.

"Yes," he replied with a chuckle. "You've heard of them, right?"

She hit him playfully with a throw pillow. "Of course. I've even had a few of them."

"So what do you say?" Ryker prompted.

Chapter 17

The laughter of the patrons in the restaurant, the sound of reggae music playing softly in the background and the delicious aroma of jerk chicken, curried goat, dumplings and other enticing entrées got Garland's senses going.

She glanced over at Ryker and found him studying her. "What?"

"You're having a good time," he responded. "I'm glad."

"I am," she confirmed. "This is a nice place. I've never been here before. Trina and I've talked about coming, but we never made it."

"This is only the second time I've been here."

Garland's awareness was heightened by Ryker's presence. She could not remember the last time she had felt this way.

"Garland, do you know what you're having?"

She loved the way her name slid off his tongue. "I'm going with the oxtail, rice and peas."

"I'm going to order the curried chicken with rice," Ryker stated.

The waiter brought them tall drinks they had ordered just a minute ago—pineapple cola with a slice of lemon and a tall straw. He then pulled out a pad and took their orders.

Garland swayed in her seat to Bob Marley's "One Love" blaring through the speakers in the background. The spectacular atmosphere was electrifying.

When the food arrived, Garland dug into her meal and savored every tasty mouthful. Nothing could beat authentic island food.

While she ate, Garland took note of how Ryker's sexy, muscular chest rose and fell.

"I noticed that we have similar tastes when it comes to TV shows," she said. "*Person of Interest* for one. I love that show."

"So do I," Ryker stated.

Garland nodded.

He took a sip of his drink. "I saw *Graceland* the other night. It looks like it might be pretty good."

"It is," she confirmed. "I've been watching it from day one."

"I see we have something else in common," Ryker stated. "Reggae music."

"Yes. I love it." She was in love with his deep, silky voice.

While they ate, they discussed favorite music, authors and charity work. They talked about so many things. It was amazing that they had so much in common.

Garland kept moving to the music as she sipped on her pineapple cola. She wondered how it was possible to be that devilishly handsome as her eyes traced his high cheekbones, thick dark eyelashes, full sensual lips healthy honey-colored complexion.

After dinner, Ryker took Garland on an evening stroll in Battery Park. The sky was a beautiful shade of blue and purple. The moon reflected on the water and a backdrop of stars sprinkled against the sky. She snuggled into his shoulder as they walked.

It was the perfect way to end the evening.

The girls were asleep when they returned home.

Ryker left Jordin and Garland alone while he went upstairs to change into a pair of sweats and a T-shirt. He'd mentioned on the drive home that it would be the first thing he did upon their arrival. Garland also suspected that he stopped at the girls' room to check on them.

"They were little angels," Jordin told her. "You two are very lucky to have those little girls."

"Sounds like you're about ready to have a family of your own," Garland responded. "You have that look."

"I am," she admitted. "I want to get married and have a little boy or girl. I've been thinking about it a lot lately, but I have to find the right man first."

"Are you seeing anyone seriously?"

Jordin shook her head. "There was a guy once who I thought would be the one, but he left town a long time ago."

Garland walked Jordin to the door. "Life is funny sometimes, so my advice to you is to never give up when it comes to love."

"Speaking out of experience, are we?" Jordin questioned while giving her a knowing glance.

Garland rolled her eyes. "Good night, Jordin. Thanks for watching the girls."

The two women embraced.

"Tell Ryker I'll see him tomorrow at the office."

"Drive safe," Garland said.

"Jordin's gone already?" Ryker asked when he walked down the stairs.

Garland nodded. "She said she'll see you tomorrow in the office."

Their gaze met and held.

Neither one of them said anything for a moment.

"I…I have some work to do before I call it a night," Ryker said.

"I guess I'll see you in the morning then," she murmured, hiding her disappointment.

Garland spent her night in her bedroom tossing, turning and feeling rejected. She craved Ryker and she thought he felt the same… They'd had a great dinner and romantic walk on the beach but that was all.

Garland could not complain. Ryker treated her like a queen and he seemed to know exactly what she wanted. She released a long sigh and turned from one side to the other. Wanting him as much as she did was pure torture.

Ryker tried not to think about the beautiful woman sleeping down the hall. He had lost a fair amount of sleep since Garland had moved in. He had been tempted to invite her into the master bedroom, but this is where he had shared so many happy moments with Angela.

A flash of memory of Angela in a pair of plaid shorts and a tank top lying back on their bed materialized in his mind. He missed her and wished for the millionth time that he could have had the chance to bid her a proper good-bye. Angela was never coming back—that part of his life was over.

Looking around the room, Ryker decided that it was

time to have it redecorated. If he and Garland were going to try to have a real marriage, then he did not want her to feel like an interloper. He wanted her to feel at home.

Ryker was grateful that Garland was not the type to pressure or try to manipulate him. She was content with giving him as much space as he needed. His body hungered for her, but he refused to use her as a receptacle for his lust. Garland deserved much more than that.

Muttering a curse, Ryker plumped up his pillow and turned on his side.

Ryker and Garland attended their first charity ball as husband and wife. Crowds of people, dressed in tuxedos and bright jewel-toned dresses, roamed through the elegant space, admiring the paintings and photographs dotting the cream-colored walls. Sculptures in metal and wood and marble stood displayed on stylish pedestals under pinpoint lighting.

Garland's short hair was a tumble of soft light brown curls that tempted Ryker to spear his fingers through its silkiness. Even in a sea of artsy, trendy people, Garland stood out wearing black. It was a stark color that accented her flawless skin. Her dress clung to curves that he ached to explore again.

When she turned, their gazes locked across the room. A flush of color stained her cheeks. Ryker thought he detected a spark of desire flash in her eyes, but he wasn't sure. Regardless, he found the thought exciting.

He almost groaned at the lurch of desire. Ryker could not help but wonder if he and Garland had a grain of hope in achieving the type of relationship required to raise their daughters. If they crossed that line into the territory of passion, he knew it would change them forever.

I can't use Garland. I care too much for her. However, when he held her close as they danced, all reason went out the window.

Chapter 18

Garland felt as if every nerve in her body was on red alert. She'd felt Ryker watching her all night and that had completely thrown her off her game. She was supposed to do her best by the local artists and, though the show had gone well overall, Garland still felt a needle of guilt because she had not been focused on her job. Instead, she had spent hours battling to keep her mind from drifting to Ryker as often as her gaze had. Why did he have to look so good?

She glanced up in time to see her mother-in-law coming her way. "Mrs. DuGrandpre, how are you?" she asked, groaning inwardly but faking a smile.

"I'm fine," Rochelle responded. "I have to say that I'm very surprised to see you here. Have you attended this event in the past?"

"Not in a couple of years," Garland answered. "However, I had a feeling you would be here tonight. We both share this passion to protect children."

"You must have been talking to Ryker."

She smiled. "He mentioned it."

"I have always believed that not everyone is meant to be a parent."

"I agree," Garland responded without emotion, but she wondered if she was referring to her?

"I see so many kids in juvenile court after horrible things have been done to them—they need protection from their family. They often become delinquents and do things to others. Then I see them in criminal court where they are doing worse things and they end up in jail or prison. It's really heartbreaking."

"Yet you don't give up," Garland stated. "You continue to fight for the children."

Rochelle nodded. "I will fight for them as long as I am able to do so."

"It's admirable of you."

"Children need gladiators." Rochelle studied her for a moment. "I'd like to know something, Garland. Why did you choose to be a single parent? You know the risks of raising a child alone."

"I should think it would be obvious. I have always wanted a child," she responded. "I admit I grew a bit impatient and decided not to wait. Surely you have to admit that there are some wonderful people in this world who were raised in single-parent homes."

Rochelle gave a slight shrug. "I guess you'd call me old-fashioned, but I believe that children need two parents."

"There are children from single-parent homes succeeding daily," Garland responded. "My father was a truck driver and hardly home except on the week-ends. My mother pretty much raised me and my brother alone and I turned out just fine." She paused a moment. "Mrs. DuGrandpre, I am devoted to both Amya and Kai—that's not going to change. Ryker knows that I am committed to raising our girls together. He is just as committed. You really don't have to worry about them. Amya and Kai have two parents who love them very much."

"You two coparent very well for now, but what happens if you meet the man of your dreams? Or my son decides he no longer wants this marriage?"

"I guess we'll have to cross that bridge when we get there, Mrs. DuGrandpre."

"These things must be considered," Rochelle stated before slipping Garland a challenging look. "There are two beautiful little girls involved. I just hope you aren't making the wrong assumptions about your relationship with my son. Because it could lead to thoughts of revenge, and I won't let you use these children as pawns."

"For the record, I haven't made any assumptions regarding your son," Garland said in a controlled voice. "As I stated earlier, Ryker and I are committed to raising our girls together. Regardless of how you or anyone else feels about our marriage, this is what we decided to do. If it fails, then Ryker and I will be the ones who will make any decisions needed at that time."

Rochelle's hackles rose and ice encased her voice and her eyes. "Taking on my family would be a huge and costly mistake."

They stood staring at each other. Garland refused to be the one to break the silence. Rochelle's tone infuriated her.

"I don't know or care what your issues are with me," Garland finally said between clenched teeth. "I'm a good mother. I also graduated at the top of my class with degrees in finance and business management. I run a successful business that I plan to expand. I don't need any of the DuGrandpre fortune. I do just fine. You will also find that I don't take well to being threatened, Mrs. DuGrandpre."

"Garland, I wondered where you'd disappeared to," Ryker stated as he joined them. "Mom, are you holding my date hostage?"

Rochelle gave a short laugh. "Of course not. We were just talking about children and the importance of good parenting."

Garland swallowed her anger. How could this woman look at her so coldly and Ryker not notice?

"Please tell me that you did not get on your soapbox."

"I didn't," his mother responded.

Ryker glanced over at Garland. "She didn't. We had a nice conversation," she lied.

Later at home, Ryker announced that it was time for another date night. "Garland, we have been so focused on the girls. This evening has convinced me that we need more adult time."

"Ryker, we're friends," she responded. "I don't mind hanging out with you. And you're right, we do need to have some time for ourselves."

He chuckled. "I know it's been a while since I've asked a woman on a date, but I didn't think I was this bad at it."

"Oh. You mean like a real date?"

"It makes sense, don't you think?" he asked. "We are

very attracted to each other. Why don't we see where this takes us?"

"Are you sure about this, Ryker?" Garland did not add that she knew he was still in love with his wife.

"I am very sure," he answered. "And for the record, I have always seen you as more than my best friend's sister. I see the woman in you. I'm sure it's no secret that my feelings for you have been growing since you and Amya moved into the house."

"We are bonding and becoming closer because of the girls," Garland stated. She wanted to make sure Ryker was not confusing his feelings. One of them had to remain rational and grounded in reality.

"I want to give our marriage a real chance," Ryker stated.

Garland nodded. "We will take it day by day. I don't want to force something that isn't there."

"Trina, I need your help," Garland said, rushing into her friend's office. "I have another date with Ryker. Can you believe it? He wants a weekly date night—real dates."

"Okay, I'm not surprised by this," she responded casually. "Why do you seem so shocked?"

"I didn't see this coming at all."

"You have feelings for the man and it's clear that he wants to be with you. What's the problem?"

"I'm not sure that this isn't about the girls, Trina. Maybe he's just afraid of losing them."

"Garland, he could think the same way about you."

"I really care for Ryker," she confessed. "But what if this doesn't work out?"

"Take it one day at a time," Trina advised.

She laughed. "I said the same thing to him just last night. I must sound like an idiot right now."

"No, not really," her friend assured her. "I understand your position. There are two innocent babies involved. It's not just about you and Ryker. I get it."

"Maybe we should keep our relationship platonic."

"Garland, if Ryker is willing to give your marriage a real chance, then you should be happy about this. You both want the same thing, so don't be so scared of letting someone get close to you."

"I'm over the heartache of relationships, Trina."

"You and Ryker live together. I really feel that this is the next step for you two."

Garland considered her words. "You're right. I just need to relax."

"Exactly."

"I'm going to do just that," she said.

"While you're at it, try and have some fun with that gorgeous hunk of a man," Trina said.

"How are things going?" Jacques asked.

"Garland and I get along really well. We actually have a date planned for tomorrow night," Ryker announced during lunch with his father.

"Why are you going through all of this?"

"I have feelings for her, Dad. Real feelings."

Jacques smiled. "Son, that's no secret. I've known that from the very beginning. Just make sure those feelings are for Garland, and you're not confusing them with what you feel for the girls."

"Dad, I hear you, but you don't have to worry about that. I really care about this woman. This is the first time

I'm saying this aloud, but I have to tell someone. I'm in love with Garland." Ryker gave a huge grin. "I love her."

"You haven't told her?"

"I want to be sure that she feels the same way about me."

"You two getting together is probably the best solution for Kai and Amya," Jacques said.

"I don't want to be with Garland just because of our daughters. I love her for who she is, Dad."

"I'm glad to hear it."

"After Angela died, I never thought I could be happy with anyone else, but Garland has given me a reason to love again. Amya and Kai are forever my babies. I am truly a grateful man."

"How long have you two been here?" Rochelle asked. She and Aubry had just arrived at the restaurant.

"Not long," Jacques said.

Aubry glanced over at her brother as she sat at the table and opened her menu. "What's going on with you these days?"

He smiled. "Same as always. Working hard and then going home and being a daddy to my two wonderful daughters. And husband to my wife."

"I need to come over and spend some time with my nieces," she said. "How is Garland?"

"She's fine," Ryker responded. "Great, in fact."

Rochelle studied his face. "What exactly is going on between you two? I was under the impression that this was just a marriage in name only—although I have been against it from the start."

His gaze did not waver. "Mom, Garland and I have genuine feelings for one another."

"Since when?"

"I have been attracted to her since we were in college. Our marriage has a real chance."

"Ryker, what in the world are you doing?" his mother questioned.

"Mom…" Aubry began. "This is his life. He can see whomever he pleases."

Rochelle sent him a sharp look. "The last thing you need to do, son, is get involved with that woman."

He leaned back in his chair and asked, "Why do you say that?"

"I don't trust her."

"Mom, not everybody is after money," Aubry stated. "This is what you're thinking, right? That Garland is after the DuGrandpre fortune."

"If you think that, then you would be wrong," Ryker stated. "Garland's store is very successful and she has her own money."

"She may be comfortable, but marrying a DuGrandpre provides an extra layer of comfort and financial security."

"You would know," Aubry uttered.

Rochelle glared at her daughter. "Excuse me?"

"You are only a DuGrandpre by marriage, Mom. Your parents weren't rich. You seem to forget that you were waitressing to help pay for law school when you met Daddy."

Stiffening, she sent her daughter a sharp glare. "So, what are you saying exactly?"

Aubry was not one to back down. "I know you love Dad, so you should know that not every woman is after money."

"What about a child?" Rochelle asked. "She may not be after money, but a child."

"I'm not going to listen to this," Ryker stated. "I'm a grown man and I'll make the decisions for my life."

"If you're not careful, Garland could end up with both girls."

"Mom, you really don't know her at all." He picked up his glass and took a long swig.

"Honey, leave it alone," Jacques said. "Ryker can handle himself."

Rochelle was clearly not happy but she kept her mouth closed. She snatched up her menu, scanning it.

Aubry met Ryker's gaze and smiled before turning her attention to the server, who had just arrived.

Chapter 19

"Thanks so much for watching the girls," Garland told Jordin. "I've already given them baths and they have their pajamas on."

"They are both so sweet and adorable. I love spending time with them."

"Amya and Kai love you," Garland said. "They were at the window looking for you a few minutes earlier."

"Joy…" Kai exclaimed.

"Hey, sweetie pie," Jordin responded. "Where's your sister?"

Kai paused and called, "Mya."

A few seconds later, Amya came running out of the bedroom. She squealed with delight when she saw Jordin.

Garland chuckled. "I guess Ryker and I can make our getaway."

"I'll take them back to the playroom until you leave," Jordin stated.

"Thanks again for babysitting."

"Don't worry about the girls. You and Ryker enjoy your evening."

Ryker came downstairs looking handsome in a tailored black suit. His eyes traveled to Garland. "You are absolutely stunning."

"You don't look too shabby yourself," she responded with a grin.

He greeted Jordin with a quick embrace. "Hello, cousin."

Jordin gently pushed him toward the door. "Go and get out of here, you two. I'm going to keep the girls busy."

Ryker took Garland's hand and led her outside of the house and into his SUV.

They had a nice evening out with good food, cold drinks and great conversation. By the time they got back to the house, the toddlers were asleep. Jordin left so that Ryker and Garland could spend the rest of the evening alone.

"I guess this means that we're stuck with each other," he teased.

"It would seem so."

Their eyes locked as their breathing seemed to come in unison.

Ryker reached over and took Garland by the hand.

A shudder heated her body at his touch.

She cleared her throat, pretending not to be affected by Ryker.

He smiled, his eyes never leaving her face.

"You're staring at me," Garland murmured.

"That's because I find you incredibly beautiful."

"Ryker, thank you for the compliment," she said. "But it's not necessary."

"You really are a breath of fresh air, Garland," he responded with a chuckle. "I've never met anyone like you before."

Their gazes locked once more and both of them could see the attraction mirrored in the other's eyes.

Ryker pulled her into his arms.

Garland drew his face to hers in a renewed embrace as her emotions whirled. He kissed her then, lingering and savoring every moment. Blood pounded in her brain, leaped from her heart and made her knees tremble.

"I have always been drawn to you, sweetheart," Ryker said. "From the moment I laid eyes on you." He touched his lips to hers again.

Garland kissed him with a hunger that belied her outward calm. She was stunned by her own eager response.

Ryker and Garland both felt the subtle shift in mood. He covered her mouth once more, kissing her passionately.

Garland eventually found the strength to pull away. Her fingers to her lips, she rushed off to her bedroom.

The next morning, Ryker forced his features to remain emotion free when Garland entered the kitchen. She was wearing a fashionable matte gold dress with a topaz-colored trim that matched her bewitching eyes to perfection. The gold and topaz sandals were a perfect match to the dress. She wore very little makeup, but she was one of few women who really did not need it.

Though Garland was trying to play it cool, Ryker could see the nerves jumping beneath her skin and the worry in her eyes. He bit back a smile. He was definitely affecting her as much as she was affecting him.

"Good morning," she said as she poured herself a cup of coffee. "What would you like for breakfast?"

"I had some toast," Ryker said. "I was about to make some oatmeal for the girls. Would you like some?"

Garland shook her head. "I've never been into oatmeal. I'll just eat a bowl of cereal."

"Are the girls up?" he asked.

"They weren't the last time I checked."

"I'll make breakfast for them while you get them up and ready for school," Ryker suggested.

Garland finished off her coffee. "Sounds like a plan." She left the kitchen, walking briskly.

When she returned, Amya and Kai were with her.

Ryker's smile brightened at the sight of his daughters. "Good morning," he said.

"Daddee," the girls said in unison.

He walked around the kitchen counter and assisted Amya into her booster seat. Garland placed Kai in hers.

"I made oatmeal," Ryker announced. "Do you want applesauce with it?"

"Abblesauce," Amya said while Kai nodded with a grin.

Garland sat at the table and, after setting bowls in front of the girls, Ryker joined her.

Her light scent drifted over to him, and he could feel his pulse race as his lower anatomy woke up. He had to find a way to get his libido back in check.

Her dress dipped in front to show the smallest hint of cleavage, increasing Ryker's desire to see more. The way it hugged her body, showing off her small waist to perfection, was exquisite torture. The oatmeal forgotten, Ryker's mouth went dry and his breathing escalated.

He spent most of his time looking at Garland's shapely legs as she crossed and recrossed them. Her sexy high-heeled shoes highlighted the beauty of her ankles.

Garland possessed the kind of legs that gave men ideas. Ryker had to snatch back his control as she unconsciously licked her lips—it was something he found incredible sexy. He was still patiently waiting for her to give him some sign that she was ready to take their relationship to the next level.

"Your breakfast is getting cold," she told him, interrupting his thoughts.

"Eat, Dayee," Kai ordered.

"I'd wondered where she got her bossiness from," Ryker said with a grin. "It all makes sense now."

"You will pay for that remark," Garland promised with a smile.

"You can't get mad at me. It's in the genes."

She laughed. "You must be talking about Parker." Garland knew that it was impossible for her daughter to inherit anything from her foster brother, but they had spent so much time together growing up, it was possible some of his qualities had rubbed off on her.

Ryker thought about it for a moment. "Yeah, he could be bossy at times, but you were always the one trying to keep us in line."

"You and my brother didn't take anything seriously. It was all about the next party."

"Until our junior year," he said. "We started to buckle down at that point."

"I wish the girls could have met him," Garland said,

then added, "What do you think he'd say about our marriage?"

"I believe he'd be happy for us." Ryker fought not to grab hold of Garland and kiss her. He craved the feel of her lips against his own.

"I'm sorry for running off the way I did last night," Garland said. "Things were getting very intense between us."

"I meant what I said about not pushing you into something you're not ready for," Ryker responded.

"I appreciate that." She checked her watch. "I need to head off to work, but I'll see you later tonight for dinner."

Ryker walked her out to the car. He met her breathtakingly intense eyes. "Have a great day," he said before kissing her gently on the lips.

"You do the same," she said with a slight grin.

"You look beautiful," Ryker said the next morning, his eyes penetrating her as he beamed. She had come downstairs with the girls just as he was about to leave for the office.

"It's sweet of you to say that, but I know the truth," Garland responded. "My hair is all over my head and I don't have any makeup on." It was her day off, so she'd thrown on a pair of denim shorts and a tank top.

"You don't need it."

"Thank you," she whispered, breathless. Garland's hormones were surging all over the place. They both gazed hungrily into each other's eyes as his intoxicating gaze seduced her.

Ryker dominated her thoughts and her heart. She felt so alive with him.

"I think you're an amazing mother." His silky, deep voice caressed her body as he watched her with the girls.

Excitement shot through Garland's body. She was dizzy with the heat of expectancy. It was an empowering experience to be treated like a queen. Every time his sexy gaze met hers, her heart turned over in response.

Slowly and seductively, Ryker's eyes slid downward. Garland's heart jolted and her pulse pounded as he pulled her close to him. She could hear his heart pound sturdily in his chest.

Clearing her throat, she pushed away and said, "Amya's so excited about starting preschool with Kai. I really think this is best because I can pick them up a little earlier now that Robyn is managing the store on the island. I've been seriously considering another store here in Charleston."

"Pickup sounds great. Sometimes I'm in court all day and it was hard trying to pick Kai up on time. Jordin and Jadin were good about helping out, but juggling schedules… It wasn't easy." Ryker picked up his car keys. "I think you should open a store here in town. It would do well."

Garland had spent her day doing laundry, running errands and grocery shopping. She found that she enjoyed taking care of her family. It was something she had longed for since she was a child—to have a real family of her own.

She even had time to squeeze in a Zumba class before picking up the girls.

Dinner was ready by the time Ryker arrived home. He gave her a warm smile.

They spent the rest of the evening with the girls before their bedtime.

"They want you to read them a story tonight," she told Ryker.

"I thought it was your turn," he teased.

Garland laughed. "Nope. They love the way you make all of the animal sounds. Have fun. I'm going to take a bubble bath."

She hoped the bath would ease some of the pent-up tension she felt. No man had ever made her feel the way Ryker made her feel—burning with desire. The way he had been able to stir her emotions, she truly believed he had to be the one for her.

Don't get ahead of yourself, she cautioned her heart.

After her bath, Garland slipped on a pair of old sweats and a cropped T-shirt. She crawled into bed and turned on the television. An image of Ryker formed in her mind, bringing a smile to her lips.

She heard footsteps in the hallway and they seemed to stop at her door.

Garland held her breath as she waited for the knock she assumed would follow.

The silence was deafening.

Had she imagined that Ryker had come to her room? Garland toyed with the idea of going to him, but her pride would not let her do so.

Ryker had made it clear he would not pressure her for sex; the man seemed to have the patience of a saint. She had thought at some point he would bring up the subject again, but thus far, he had been true to his word.

She tossed a small pillow across the room in frustration. Ryker was forever the honorable gentleman.

Garland eventually found something interesting to watch.

An hour into the movie, her eyes grew heavy, forcing Garland to turn off the television.

She fell asleep almost instantly.

When Garland opened her eyes, she sat up in bed and glanced over at the clock. It was five minutes after six—almost time to get up. She shut down the alarm clock to keep it from going off and then eased out of bed.

Garland had spent most of the night dreaming about Ryker. Her heart skipped a beat at the mere memory. As she brushed her teeth, realization dawned on her.

I'm in love with Ryker.

Garland managed to get ready for work. She took care to pick out a suit, deciding to wear a red and black color-block jacket over a pair of black pants.

Standing in front of her mirror, she fingered the soft curls in her hair, separating them.

Ryker opened the door to the master bedroom and stepped into the hallway within seconds of her leaving her room.

"Good morning," they said in unison before bursting into laughter.

"You look nice," he told her.

"Thank you," Garland responded. "I'm going in early today so that I can pick up the girls from school around four. I want to take them to see the puppet show at the children's museum this afternoon."

"If I can clear my schedule, I'll meet you there."

"That would be nice, but if you can't, Ryker, it's okay. We'll just see you later tonight."

"I'm glad that you're here."

Garland chuckled. "You tell me that a lot."

"It's because I mean it and I want you to know how much I appreciate you. You understand how important it is for me to keep Kai in my life. I feel she is just as much my child as she is yours."

"I know that," she responded. "I feel the exact same way about Amya." There was more she wanted to say, but the time just wasn't right.

Chapter 20

Later that evening, Ryker watched as Garland crawled around on the floor with the girls. He loved hearing them laugh.

A touch of sadness overtook him. How he wished Parker could be here to see the woman his sister had become. Ryker also wished that Angela could have had the chance to meet her daughter.

Garland looked up and saw him. She waved.

He felt guilty about her, too. Garland deserved the love of a good man—not a man mourning for his dead wife. But the thought of her with someone other than him struck a jealous chord within him. He could no longer deny the truth. Ryker wanted Garland for himself.

"Hey, can I play, too?" he asked as he dropped to his knees.

"Yessh," Kai answered. She stretched out her arms, reaching for him. "Dayee."

Giggling, Amya threw her arms around his legs.

"We are so lucky to have been blessed with two darling daughters," Garland said as she crawled over to him. They sat side by side near the fireplace.

He embraced her. "Yes, we are."

She gave Ryker a sidelong look. "Sometimes I feel like this is a dream and I'm going to wake up one day and discover that none of this is real."

He leaned over and kissed her gently on the lips. "It's very real, I assure you."

They played for a little while longer before Garland announced it was time for bed.

After they settled the girls in bed, Ryker and Garland went back downstairs.

"Are you in the mood for a swim?" he asked.

"Sure," she responded.

"Put on your swimsuit and meet me downstairs in five."

Singing softly, she rushed up to her room.

Ryker was waiting for her near the French doors leading to the patio. When she came down in her black swimsuit, he swallowed hard and led them outside to the pool.

"The water feels good," Garland said.

She swam from one end of the pool to the other.

He watched her a moment before joining her for the second lap.

"Are you still going to sign the girls up for swimming lessons?" he asked her after they climbed out of the pool."

"I'd like to," Garland replied.

"It's fine with me."

She glanced up at the sky. "It's really beautiful out here. I love nights like this when the moon is full."

Ryker sat still, absorbing what she'd said.

Garland gave him an indirect glance. "This is such a perfect night."

He pulled her to her feet. "You're right," he said. "Everything about this night is perfect."

Kissing her, Ryker backed her up until her legs hit the poolside table, and she stood pressed up against the hard surface. There was no escape.

Garland's breath quickened, making her breasts rise and fall faster as they brushed against his chest. Her cheeks were flushed, and her lips were swollen from his kisses.

It was clear that Garland wanted him, but she was fighting herself as much as she was fighting him.

Ryker did not just want her. He needed her.

He felt a low growl rumble in his throat, and then he crushed his lips against hers. Grabbing her neck to pull her closer, he pushed his tongue against her lips, demanding entrance.

Garland reached her hand up to push him away, but instead she ended up gripping his back. She could not stop her body's betrayal as she melted against him. He penetrated her mouth and then tangled his tongue with hers.

Liquid heat began pooling in her core as Ryker deepened the kiss and pulled her so close to his hard chest that she could hardly tell where her body left off and his began. Her hands slipped up behind his neck.

Ryker could not think beyond anything but his need. He was hungry, and only Garland could satisfy him.

He broke the kiss long enough to trail his lips down her neck. Fire ran through him as he reconnected with the first girl he'd ever cared about.

"I want to make love to you," he whispered against her cheek. "I need you."

His words sent new spirals of ecstasy through her and she could not refuse him.

He traced a fingertip across her lip.

"I need to hear you say it," he whispered. "Tell me that you want me as bad as I want you."

"I want you," Garland whispered as she pulled him closer.

Without another word, Ryker led her through the house, up to the second level and into the master bedroom.

Later as they lay entangled in damp sheets, Ryker stroked her arm, saying, "I want you to move into this room with me permanently. You're my wife and I want to wake up with you beside me."

She pulled the covers to her chest. "Maybe you should take a day or two and think about this, Ryker. I want you to be sure of your decision."

"I've given this a lot of thought, Garland. I want us to have a real marriage." He had already removed Angela's photo from the nightstand and placed it in a photo album. It was time for him to build a life with the woman living in his home.

Ryker took Garland to High Cotton on East Bay Street for date night.

"So you've eaten here before?" he asked when she suggested that he try the shrimp and grits.

"Once with my mom for her birthday, but this is the first time I've ever been in one of their private rooms. I can't believe that you booked this entire room just for us. This is nice," Garland said. Her eyes bounced around the room draped in rich but soothing jewel tones. For the first time since they'd gotten married, she felt like a woman having dinner with her husband.

"I'm glad you like it," he responded. "For our entrées I ordered the jumbo lump crab cakes with jalapeño rémoulade for you and the shrimp and grits for me. I remembered how much you love seafood and spicy foods in general."

She was touched by his thoughtfulness. The fact that he remembered the little things offered her hope for the future.

Waiters began bringing the first course out, arranging the soup, crab and salads attractively on the table.

"Wow," she murmured. "This looks so delicious."

Ryker gestured with his fork. "Try the soup."

They continued to talk while they enjoyed their meal.

Garland was beyond happy. She loved waking up beside Ryker each morning, and making love to him was everything she'd ever imagined it would be.

Her life was perfect.

"I love seeing you so happy," Ryker said, cutting into her thoughts.

She smiled. "I have two beautiful daughters and a wonderful husband who is also my friend. I have every reason to be happy."

Ryker covered her hand with his own. "I feel the same way, sweetheart. I'm beginning to believe that this is the way it was supposed to be from the very beginning. You and I belong together."

Garland wanted to believe Ryker meant everything he said. He still loved Angela, but perhaps there was some room left in his heart for her.

The following week, Garland made the girls a good dinner when they arrived home and then tossed a ball with them in the backyard. She loved it when Charleston's weather saw fit to cooperate and she could spend time outdoors with her daughters.

They played outside until Ryker arrived home.

"What did I miss?" he asked when they entered the house through the French doors.

"We were out playing ball," Garland responded. "I thought it might be enough exertion to allow them both a good night's sleep. I've already fed them. I thought maybe you and I could have a quiet, romantic dinner together."

He smiled. "I like that idea."

She broke into a grin. "It's almost ready."

They discussed their day as they dined on a garden salad, shrimp scampi over linguini and chocolate-covered strawberries for dessert.

"When I pulled into the garage, I couldn't wait to open the door and take in the delicious smells of dinner cooking, hear my daughter's laughter and plant a kiss on you. It just feels normal."

"I always imagined that life was much easier when you're married," Garland responded.

"How do you feel about it now?" he asked, meeting her gaze.

Garland broke into a grin. "My theory is correct. I wasn't sure that you were in this for the long haul until we made love. I felt like that was a commitment to our marriage."

"I am very committed to our marriage, but I didn't want to push you into sharing my bed until you were ready to give yourself to me."

Their eyes met and she smiled with dawning warmth.

The evening ended with Ryker leading his wife upstairs to their bedroom.

His hands explored the hollows of her back. His breath was hot against her ear.

When he touched her skin, it tingled to the point that she thought she might faint with desire.

Ryker leaned down to Garland and captured her lips again as he inched closer. His lips parted and claimed her tongue. Hungrily, they devoured each other's lips, which left Garland melting into his passionate embrace.

Her entire body pulsated in anticipation. Ryker tenderly kissed her on the throat as he traced his fingertips across her lips. The gentle massage sent currents of desire through her. She hungered for his taste.

Their chemistry was electrifying. Garland's last thought before she drifted to sleep was just how perfect she and Ryker were together.

Chapter 21

"Is someone here?" Garland whispered sleepily.

Ryker shifted his body and groaned. "Oops. I forgot my parents were coming by this morning."

She hopped out of bed and rushed into the bathroom just minutes before Rochelle knocked on the bedroom door.

"Son, are you okay?"

"I'm fine. Just give us a minute to get dressed. We'll be down in a moment."

His words were met by dead silence.

"How could you forget they were coming over?" Garland questioned when she walked out of the bathroom wearing a robe. "I am so embarrassed."

"You were the only person I was thinking about," Ryker confessed as he slipped on a pair of sweats and a T-shirt. "You don't have any reason to be embarrassed. We're man and wife."

Garland quickly dressed in a pair of leggings and an oversize T-shirt. She ran her fingers through her hair, fluffing her curls.

When they walked out of the bedroom, they heard Rochelle in the girls' room, talking and laughing with them. Ryker headed in that direction, followed by Garland.

His mother eyed them both before saying, "We should have called first. I'm sorry for just barging in. Your father and I had no idea you two would be sleeping in."

"Maybe you should just call to confirm from now on," Ryker suggested.

Rochelle sent him a sharp glare but did not respond.

"I'll get the girls dressed," Garland said.

"It's nice of you to join us, Garland," Rochelle uttered.

"Mrs. DuGrandpre, I'm afraid I had no idea that you were coming by," she responded. There was something about her mother-in-law that bothered Garland. She was not sure what it was—maybe it was the intense stare down or the smile that never quite seemed sincere.

They joined Ryker and his father in the family room. Rochelle sank down beside Jacques while Garland joined Ryker on the loveseat.

"The girls look happy," Rochelle stated.

"They are," Garland confirmed. "Kai and Amya are very happy and they have adapted well to our arrangement."

Rochelle nodded with pursed lips. "Good to hear. By the way, I'm coming to Edisto Island tomorrow," she announced. "Why don't we have lunch together?"

"Sure," Garland responded with a slight nod. "That would be nice."

* * *

"I hope my mother didn't upset you during her visit earlier."

"She didn't."

"Good. Well, don't let her get to you, Garland," Ryker advised. "I've learned that you have to set boundaries with my mother. She means well but has a hard time staying in her lane from time to time."

"I'll have to remember that, but I think she's getting better. Remember that she invited me to have lunch with her tomorrow. This will give us a chance to really get to know one another."

He nodded.

"I'm actually looking forward to it," Garland said. "Hopefully, this is a brand-new start for your mother and me."

"I'm so glad we were able to get together for lunch," Rochelle stated after she and Garland were seated. "We can have a lovely chat over a delicious meal."

"I have to confess that I was a bit surprised you wanted to get together," she said. "I didn't think you cared for me."

"It's not anything like that at all. It is not that I don't like you, dear. My concern is merely for my granddaughters."

Folding her napkin across her lap, Garland said, "I hope that you are more comfortable now with my marriage to Ryker."

Rochelle met her gaze. "But what happens after this *marriage* runs its course? What happens to the girls?"

"Ryker and I will always be here for our daughters," Garland replied. "That will never change."

"It's easy for you to say that now. I'm sure that you know breakups bring out the worse in people."

Garland remained silent.

"My son has been through a lot, as you know. He can't lose his daughters."

Garland laid the menu down in front of her. "What are you getting at, Mrs. DuGrandpre?"

"It would be better for you to give Ryker sole custody of the girls. After all, he can generously provide for them. If this little pretend marriage between you two does not work out...well, then it's all for the better."

"I am not going to give up my children. Ryker and I can share joint custody, if it comes to that, but I'm never giving him sole custody."

"I don't think you'll have any choice, Garland."

"What do you mean by that?"

"Ryker is a very wealthy man and you could exploit that, which is why he has papers ready for you to sign in the event the marriage ends in divorce," Rochelle announced. "I know that you believe you are equipped to raise Kai and Amya, but you can't give them what we can. You might as well know that I advised my son to do this before the wedding."

The sting of betrayal pierced Garland. "Ryker has never mentioned any of this to me. Even if he had, I would've made it clear that I would fight him with every breath in my body for those girls. I may not have millions of dollars and my house may be the square footage of his bedroom, but none of that means anything. I am a good mother."

She and Ryker had been living together all this time and he'd never once said a word. Garland was livid.

"Ryker is also a very good father and he loves those

girls," Rochelle pointed out. "I told him I would handle it…as his attorney. Garland, let's be honest. I know that you are a nice young woman, but you are not the one for my son. He is with you out of some misguided loyalty to your brother. In the long run, neither of you will be happy in a loveless marriage."

"What Ryker and I share has nothing to do with Parker," Garland managed to reply.

"Garland, dear, you have a lot on your hands with your mother and your business. Just let Ryker have the girls. It's not like you won't be able to visit them."

"Mrs. DuGrandpre, this conversation is over," Garland stated. "I will talk to Ryker about the girls and these documents."

"I am his attorney. You will deal with me."

"I really don't want to disrespect you, but if you keep pushing, that's exactly what's going to happen. Your son and I decided to work this out without legal representation. If he changed his mind, then he should be the one sitting here and talking to me. *I will deal with Ryker and only him.*"

The waiter approached the table.

"I'm afraid I won't be able to stay," Garland said, rising to her feet. "Enjoy your lunch."

"If you would put your feelings aside, you'd know I am doing the right thing. Just think about what I've said," Rochelle said. "Think of the girls and their happiness."

"It's amazing how you can manage to take care of your clients while interfering in the lives of your children," Garland snapped in anger as she walked out of the restaurant.

* * *

Her conversation with Rochelle was still at the forefront of her mind when Garland pulled into the driveway of her and Ryker's home. Garland did not believe Rochelle entirely and she wanted to prove her wrong.

She headed straight into his home office. Garland did not like being a snoop, but she needed to find out if Ryker deserved her trust. And on the corner of his desk she caught sight of a manila folder.

Unable to resist temptation, Garland opened it.

She gasped in shock and tears filled her eyes.

The documents were a copy of the ones Rochelle had waved in her face. Apparently, she did not know Ryker as well as she thought she did.

A photo fell out of the stack of papers. Garland pulled it out and held it beneath the light to gaze at the image. It was of Parker, Ryker and her the summer before their senior year.

Garland forced herself to put away the worn photo. This was no time for old memories. The sooner she saw Ryker, the sooner she'd get the answers she needed.

"This is a pleasant surprise," Ryker said with his trademark smile when Garland blew into his downtown office without knocking.

Dropping her purse into one of the empty chairs, she uttered, "You're going to think different when I say what I have to say."

"Is something wrong?"

"Yes," Garland fired back. "*Something is very wrong.* I thought I could trust you of all people, Ryker."

"I'm confused. What's going on?"

"I saw the papers."

Ryker merely shrugged at her. "What papers?"

"The agreement or whatever you want to call it. You know the one that states that I will give you sole custody of the girls in the event we decide to end our marriage."

Ryker eyed her. "I honestly have no idea what you're talking about, Garland."

"How can you lie to my face? The papers were in your office at home. I saw them."

"Garland, I've never had any papers drawn up."

"If you think you can take those girls from me, I will fight you until I take my very last breath."

"Honey, calm down," he pleaded.

"I'm moving out and I'm taking Amya with me," Garland announced. "I can't live with someone I can't trust."

Before she had the chance to take a few steps, Ryker rose to his feet, walked around his desk and grabbed her arm. She was suddenly standing too close to him. His smell was invading her senses, making the heat pool in her core.

"Don't do this, Garland." The second Ryker touched her arm, lightning shot through his fingertips, straight to his groin. "You are my wife and—"

At that moment his mother blew into the office without knocking. "What in the world is going on in here? Everyone can hear you in the hallway," Rochelle admonished. "Keep your voices down!"

"You know exactly what is going on in here," Garland told Rochelle.

Ryker stared at his mother. "Are you responsible for this?" he asked, holding up the legal documents in his hand.

"I'm only looking out for the children," she told him.

"This woman is not the one for you and I'm not going to let you bind yourself to her just because of a child."

"Mom, I love you, but you have no right to interfere in my life."

"I'll leave you to deal with your mommy issues," Garland stated. "But I think that maybe she's right this time. We should explore our legal options."

"I will not have the girls separated," he said. "My mother has nothing to do with this."

"They are my grandchildren," Rochelle argued. "If you're not careful, you are going to end up losing both girls."

"Mom, this is between me and Garland. Please leave."

"I—"

"I want you to leave my office," Ryker ordered. "I will talk to you later. You can count on that."

"She can stay," Garland interjected, her hands clenched at her sides while she tried to pull herself together. "I'm the one who's leaving."

"We need to finish our discussion."

"There really isn't anything to talk about."

"We have a lot to discuss."

Garland shook her head. "This was never going to work out for us. I don't know you, Ryker."

She grabbed her purse and took quick steps across the carpeted floor. "Right now I'm too disgusted with you and your mother to stay here any longer."

Garland made what she deemed a dignified exit, but as soon as she left Ryker's office, she raced down the hallway and into the ladies' room, where she cried hysterically.

After she gained her composure, she slowly made her way to her car. Garland allowed herself a total of about five minutes to pull herself together enough to make the drive to the school to pick up the girls and take them home.

The day felt as if it had been the longest of her life. How was she going to keep her self-control for the rest of the afternoon, let alone the evening?

Her heart had been broken before; it was not such a big deal. Besides, Garland acknowledged, she was healthy enough to move forward alone if necessary. She took a deep breath.

By the time Garland pulled into the three-car garage, she had banished Ryker from her current thoughts; however, he continued to linger in the back of her mind. Each time he tried to take over, Garland pushed him back into the recesses again. It did not help knowing that she would have a terrible time now getting rid of him. After all, Ryker was the father of her children. He was the one with all of the money and the power.

In reality, what could she do if he decided to sue for full custody of the girls? He had no legal rights to Kai, but she wouldn't tear her daughter out of his arms like that.

After the girls went to their room to play before dinner, Garland slid down to the hallway floor outside of their room, fighting the urge to sob out of anger and frustration. She did not want the girls raised separately but she had no other choice.

"You did the right thing by letting her leave. Don't go running after her now," Rochelle urged when Ryker headed toward the door. "Son, she's not the woman for you. Why can't you see that?"

"I am a grown man," he snapped in anger. "You can't control my life. When are you going to understand that?"

"Garland has blindsided you."

"She has done nothing but be a good…no, great mother to our daughters. How could you go behind my back and have custody papers drawn up?" When their eyes collided, Ryker felt as if he had been punched in the gut. "Aubry's right. You know nothing about boundaries."

"I was only trying to help."

"No, you weren't," Ryker countered. "You were trying to control this situation like everything else."

Rochelle blew her breath out in frustration. "You don't know women—"

"I know Garland. I've known her for a long time and she's not manipulative. You are the one who's been doing the manipulating if we're to be honest."

"It's obvious there's nothing I can say to you to make you understand."

"You're right about that." It was time to put his mother in her place.

Ryker packed up his laptop. "Did it ever occur to you that I am in love with Garland? She is the woman I want to spend the rest of my life with, Mom. If you've ruined this for me, I'm not sure I'll be able to forgive you. I could even lose one of my daughters behind what you've done."

"She means this much to you?" Rochelle asked, clearly stunned by his words.

"Yes, she does."

Her shoulders slumped, and Ryker was surprised not to feel joy at her defeat. Then she said quietly, "Would you like for me to go talk to her?"

Ryker shook his head. "That's the last thing I want

from you. I'd rather you stay as far away from her as possible."

"You don't have to be so rude, son."

"It seems it's the only way we can get you to understand anything, Mom." He brushed past her and walked toward the door. "I need to find my wife."

Chapter 22

Garland wiped away a lone tear as she packed her suit-case. She had changed into a pair of sweatpants and a sports bra. She had little energy to care about her looks.

"I don't want you to leave," Ryker said from the door-way. "You're my wife, Garland, and I want a real marriage with you."

"We can't always have everything that we want," she uttered in response. Garland was hurt and angry.

She removed a stack of shirts out of a drawer. "You didn't need to come home. I can move out all by myself."

"I didn't have those papers drawn up. Why won't you believe me?"

She met his gaze. "It really doesn't matter anymore, Ryker. Your mother doesn't like me and I'm not going through life with her constant interference."

"I know that she's controlling and manipulative, but

she is still my mother and I love her. And she is Amya's grandmother."

Garland shrugged. "You have to deal with your mother. I don't."

"Yes, you do," Ryker argued. "Garland, you are a member of this family whether you like it or not."

"Can't you see that this isn't going to work out between us? The writing's all over the wall, Ryker."

"Why do you believe that?" he asked.

"Because I'm a realist, Ryker. We wanted it to work because of the girls."

"I wanted it to work because I want us—all of us—to be a family."

"Why can't you just be honest with me, Ryker? This is only about the girls."

"Stop saying that," he uttered. "Garland, it's not true. Maybe in the beginning, but you know that things have changed between us. And I've made sure that my mother won't be bothering you again."

"You think it's going to be that easy?" she asked him.

"Garland, please give us a chance."

"I can't stay here right now. I need some time to think."

"Why do you have to take Amya?"

"I don't trust your mother. Right now, I just want to go home. It's a safe place for me and Amya. I would take Kai with us, but I know you'd object."

"You're right. I'm not happy about Amya leaving, either."

"I need to do this, Ryker. This will give you some time to think about our marriage, too."

"I can move into the guest bedroom," he told her. "You don't have to leave the house."

"Ryker, we need some time apart. We rushed into

this marriage. I'm not trying to rush into a divorce, but I just need time alone—I need to be away from you."

Garland pulled the folds of her sweater together as she and Ryker wandered along the beach in tense silence. She had been away from the house for almost a week before he'd driven out to talk to her. He had called daily to check on Amya, however.

"Cold?" he asked, breaking the tension.

"It's a little brisk out here, but I'm fine," she responded.

"I have to admit that I never saw this day coming. We were supposed to be enjoying our life together."

Garland glanced over at him. "I didn't see this, either."

He stopped walking. "It doesn't have to be this way, sweetheart."

"Ryker, don't do this."

"Kai is upset. She doesn't understand why you and Amya aren't there. She's been having accidents again."

Garland stopped in her tracks. "You think it's my fault?"

"I think blame can be placed on both of us," he responded. "How has Amya been?"

"She wants to see you and Kai. She said 'sister' for the first time today.

"Ryker, I need to know something," Garland began, "and I want you to be honest with me. Would you really fight me for the girls?" She could hardly look at him because she was hurting so badly.

His silence seemed to be the answer to her question.

Garland had done the best possible job she could as a mother. But Ryker had the money for the best attorneys—he had his mother in his corner and she was the best family law attorney in all of South Carolina. If they ended up in court, Ryker would probably win. Deep down, Garland felt defeated and devastated.

Finally, Ryker answered. "Sweetheart, I would never fight you for custody. If things do not work out with our marriage, we will always share joint custody and work on being the best parents we can be," he responded. "I'm sorry my mother put you through this mess, but I give you my word—it won't happen again." He paused a moment. "Come home, Garland. I won't take you to court. I won't hurt the children by keeping them away from you. You should know that I'm not that kind of man."

Ryker was not doing this for her, Garland realized. This was strictly about the girls. Sadly, she shook her head. "I think your mother is right, Ryker. I'm not the type of woman a DuGrandpre marries. More importantly, I know that you have not gotten over Angela. You may have taken off the wedding band, but your heart still belongs to her."

"Garland, talking about Angela has not been easy for me, but I'm ready now. I want to tell you about her."

She almost objected, but remained quiet, watching the expression of anguish on his face.

"Angela loved life and loved people. No matter where we went, she'd always run into someone she knew. Sometimes she would just strike up a conversation with a complete stranger."

"She sounds pretty special."

He smiled. "When they told me she was dead, I didn't believe it. I kept staring at her, waiting for her to open her eyes and give me that huge smile of hers. Only she didn't." Ryker swallowed hard. "They worked to deliver Kai…no, Amya, safely, and then things happened so quickly. They took the baby to the nursery and gave me some time to say good-bye."

Garland took his hand in hers. "I'm so sorry."

"A part of me was angry with Angela for leaving me. We—*she*—had made all of these plans for our daughter, but she never even got to meet her. Instead, I was left with a new baby and no knowledge of how to be a father."

"No one is born knowing how to be a parent, sweetheart," she said in a low tone. "It's trial and error."

"When you came back into my life, I had so many mixed emotions. I felt guilty for being angry with her leaving and guilty for having feelings for you. Since I'm being honest, I think I fell in love with you the day we saw each other at the hospital. I just wasn't ready to acknowledge it."

"Ryker, I'm not sure you really know what you feel," Garland fired back. "I know that you're attracted to me, but it's not love. Each time we've made love, you tell me how much you *want* me, but what I really needed was to hear you tell me how much you *loved* me." She sighed. "Those words never once came out of your mouth and it's okay. I went into a physical relationship with you with my eyes wide-open, Ryker."

He pulled her into his arms. "I'm sorry I failed you, Garland. I am a deliberate man and I like to be sure before I make a declaration like that. I need you to hear me. Sweetheart, I love you and I don't want to lose you."

After a moment, she asked, "Are you sure? What about Angela?"

"I loved Angela and if she were still alive, I'd like to believe that we would still be together, but she's gone,"

Ryker admitted. "Part of me will always regret that she never met Amya or had a chance to be a mother, but I am so grateful to have you and Kai in my life. I am a lucky man because I have the three of you. Now, I need to know something from you. Do you love me, Garland?"

"I love you, Ryker. I'm just not sure it's enough. I don't want to experience this kind of heartache ever again."

"Garland, I want to spend the rest of my life with you. I really hope that you can forgive me and my mother for the hurt we've caused you. I promise I will spend the rest of my life making this up to you."

She looked up at him with an expression of hope. "Do you mean what you just said?"

"Yes," Ryker responded. "I love you so much."

Garland fell into his arms, mumbling against his neck. "I should have trusted you. I'm so sorry I didn't."

"I can understand how upsetting it could be to see those documents, but I tore them up and ordered my mother to stop interfering in our marriage or she will risk not being able to see her grandchildren."

Ryker slowly drew her more tightly into his arms.

"We should get back to the house," Garland said, her heart bursting with pure happiness. "Trina's dropping off Amya and I know she would love to see you."

"I want to see her, too. The girls are too young to be bounced back and forth like this. We have to be in this marriage for better or worse, Garland. If you have any doubts about me or my feelings for you—now is the time to get them all out. I don't want to put the girls through this a second time."

She placed her hand in his. "I agree, Ryker."

He kissed her. "I missed you so much, sweetheart.

Kai missed you just as much. She kept looking for you. It broke my heart."

"I'm sorry," Garland murmured. "Running away was not the answer. If I wanted to leave, I never should've taken Amya with me, but I wanted to hurt you because I was hurting. It was childish and I hope you will be able to forgive me, Ryker."

"There is nothing to forgive. We were both manipulated by my mother, but it won't happen again."

"Daddee," Amya screamed when she saw him sitting in the living room. "Ooh Daddee…"

Garland's eyes teared up at the sight of her daughter clinging to Ryker for dear life.

"Oh, sweet baby…" Ryker said. His watery gaze traveled to Garland.

Trina wrapped an arm around her friend and whispered, "You need to go back home, sweetie. You can't work things out with Ryker if you're here on Edisto Island and he's in Charleston. I can see how much you two love each other. Go home with your husband."

Garland nodded.

"I'll pack a bag for Amya."

They embraced. "Thanks, Trina."

She walked over to Ryker and announced, "We're coming back to the house. Trina's packing a bag for Amya. Why don't you take her with you and I'll be there in about an hour? I need to take care of some things before I head back to Charleston."

"Thank you," he responded.

"I'm going to sleep in the guest room tonight," she announced when she arrived at the house in Charleston.

"I'm just glad that you're back home where you belong," Ryker replied. "But you are not sleeping in the guest room. You are my wife and I want you sleeping beside me as it should be."

"Are you sure about this?" she asked. Garland was surprised by Ryker's willingness to just forgive her after she had taken his daughter away.

With so much weighing heavy on her mind, Garland figured she would climb into bed and lie there awake all night. Instead, her heavy eyes closed and oblivion quickly overtook her.

The next morning, Ryker surprised her with breakfast in bed.

She spied a small box on the tray. "What's this?" Garland asked, her curiosity getting the best of her.

"Open it."

She did as he requested.

A gasp escaped her lips as she eyed the two-carat, cushion-cut engagement ring with a matching diamond-encrusted wedding band. "Ryker…it's gorgeous."

"You told me that you didn't want me to give you a ring until our marriage was real. This is proof that what we share between us is real and proof that I am committed to you for all of eternity." Placing the ring on her left hand, he said, "This is what this ring symbolizes."

Garland smiled as she reached into the drawer on her nightstand and pulled out a black velvet box. "I bought this for you a couple of weeks ago. I was waiting for the right time." She opened it to reveal a platinum and diamond wedding band. "I wanted to give this to you when you were ready to give your heart to me. A marriage cannot grow stronger and better without love." She placed the ring on his finger.

"It's not too late for me to give you the wedding of your dreams," Ryker said.

Garland shook her head. "I'm perfectly satisfied with the ceremony we had. We don't need to spend thousands of dollars on one day when we've got two daughters to send to college—at the same time, I might add."

"Our daughters have trust funds," Ryker told her. "We don't have to worry about college tuition."

Garland shrugged. " Ryker, you're my husband and as far as I'm concerned, it doesn't get any better than this. However, it might be nice to plan a honeymoon since we never really had one. Some place exotic and very romantic."

He grinned. "I like the sound of that."

A week after they returned from their honeymoon in Aruba, Garland met Ryker at the firm for a lunch date. While she was there, Rochelle came to the office. Garland knew things were still very tense between her mother-in-law and husband.

As angry as she was with Rochelle, Garland also hated the gap in the mother and son's once-close relationship.

Without glancing up from his computer monitor, he uttered, "Mom, what do you want? My wife and I are just about to head out for lunch."

"I don't intend to keep you long, but there's something I need to say to you both."

"What is it now?" he asked.

"Ryker, I came here to apologize to you," she stated. "I heard everything you said and I was wrong for trying to break up you and Garland. I give you my word that I won't interfere in your marriage ever again."

He met her gaze straight on. "It's a little too late, don't you think?" he asked. "The damage has already been done. I'm just thankful I didn't lose Garland."

"Honey, I was only trying to look out for you. I did not realize that you had fallen in love with her."

"How many times do I need to tell you that I don't need you to protect me?" Ryker uttered. "I can take care of myself."

"You're absolutely right," Rochelle responded. Turning to Garland, she said, "I hadn't realized just how much you love my son."

Garland met Rochelle's gaze straight on. "Yes, I love him with everything that is in me."

"Despite my actions, I'm glad that Ryker has found love again," she said. "It's all that I ever wanted for him and Aubry. I want my children to find the same kind of love that I share with their father."

"I get it," Garland told her. "But the heart chooses who it wants to love—not you."

Rochelle nodded. "Once more, I just came here to apologize to you for my actions. I promise to stay out of your marriage and I mean it."

"Mrs. DuGrandpre," Garland began, "I need you to know that I have never been interested in the DuGrandpre's money and I'm willing to sign a legal document stating as much. I love Ryker and our children—as long as we're happy and healthy, that's all that matters to me."

Rochelle offered a tiny smile. "I have misjudged you, Garland, and I'm woman enough to admit when I'm wrong. I hope that you can one day forgive me."

Garland smiled. "That day is today. I really would like for us to work on being friends, Mrs. DuGrandpre."

"Honey, we are family, so no more of the formality. Call me Mom or Rochelle—whichever makes you comfortable."

The two women embraced.

"How about I take you ladies to lunch?" Ryker suggested. "Aubry has a new test menu that she wants to try out on the family."

"Sounds good to me," Garland said with a smile.

Later that evening, she padded barefoot out of the bathroom, smelling of lavender.

Ryker eyed the silk boxer shorts and tank top she was wearing. He strode quickly, meeting her near the king-size bed.

"You won't be needing these tonight."

She gave him a sexy grin. "You won't be needing anything on, either. Did you lock the door?"

Ryker nodded. "And I checked on the girls and they are fast asleep."

Garland wrapped her arms around him and said, "I almost messed things up between us. I'm so glad you came after me."

"How could I not?" he asked. "We vowed before God and our family that we were in this marriage together for better or for worse. I meant every word."

"I have loved you for so long," Garland whispered. "I just didn't realize it until our wedding day."

Epilogue

"I can't believe that our daughters are four years old today," Garland told Ryker as they prepared for Amya and Kai's birthday celebration. She handed him a balloon to hang from the ceiling. "Our babies are growing up so fast."

He agreed. "Amya told me this morning that she was not a baby anymore. She said that she's a big girl now." Ryker hung the last balloon and then followed his wife into the kitchen.

Garland laughed. "Oh, really?"

"Yeah. I was trying to help her with her backpack and she told me that she didn't need my help. I have to be honest—my feelings were hurt just a little."

Standing beside him, Garland openly admired Ryker as he removed the cupcakes from the oven. She loved Ryker more than life itself and never tired of looking at him. He was not only handsome and muscular, he also had a generous heart.

"Are you finished with the hamburger patties?" he asked.

"Almost," she responded. Garland had forgotten what she was doing—she had gotten so caught up in eyeing her husband of nearly two years.

Smiling, she handed him the platter of raw meat. "All ready for the grill."

"Thanks, sweetheart," he responded. "I'll take these out to Dad. He's got it all fired up and ready."

"When will your mother be back with the girls?" Garland's relationship with her mother-in-law had improved as they found they had a lot in common, including their passion for the plight of disadvantaged children. In fact, she and Rochelle were working together to form a foundation to help promote foster parenting.

Jadin, Jordin and their parents arrived bearing birthday gifts for the girls.

"I told Ryker not to worry about making anything," Aubry said when she walked into the kitchen. "Those cupcakes do look delicious, though."

"When did you get here?" Garland asked.

"About ten minutes ago. I was on the patio talking to Daddy. I put the cake in the refrigerator."

"Thanks for all of your help, Aubry. The girls are going to love the castle cake."

"It's almost time for Mom to bring them back," she announced. "Angela's parents are here and some of the kids from their school. You should go get dressed."

"Ryker should be down in a few minutes," Garland said before heading upstairs, humming softly.

Everything was going as planned. She wanted Amya

and Kai to have the birthday party of their dreams. They both wanted a castle-shaped cake and everyone to dress like princes and princesses. Ryker and Garland were the king and queen.

She laughed at the thought. She doubted members of royalty dined on hamburgers, hot dogs and grilled chicken.

Garland entered the master bedroom and burst into laughter.

"I can't believe I have to wear this crown and cape thing," Ryker said.

"At least you don't have to wear tights," she reminded him. "Although they would look much better with the boots than your jeans do."

Ryker shook his head. "Tights are completely out of the question."

Laughing, Garland quickly slipped into a purple gown with silver trim.

After they had served birthday cake to everyone, Garland walked up to her husband and handed him a cupcake with a candy pacifier on top of it.

"What's this?" Ryker gazed into her eyes as they shared a meaningful look. "Are you…"

She nodded. "I am. We're having a baby."

They burst into joyous laughter.

"After all that's happened, I'm thinking we should have this baby at home," Ryker stated. "Don't you agree?"

Garland shook her head. "We are going to have this baby in a hospital where they have lots of pain medication. I know they have the electronic bracelets that will lock down the hospital if someone tries to take the baby, but I don't care. We are not going to let this child out of our sight."

"Agreed," he responded with a smile. Placing a hand to her stomach, he whispered, "Forever my baby."

* * * * *

It may be the biggest challenge she's ever faced...

NAUGHTY

National Bestselling Author
ROCHELLE ALERS

Parties, paparazzi, red-carpet catfights and shocking sex tapes—wild child Breanna Parker has always used her antics to gain attention from her R & B–diva mother and record-producer father. But now, as her whirlwind marriage to a struggling actor implodes, Bree is ready to live life on her own terms, and the results will take everyone—including Bree—by surprise.

"Rochelle Alers is the African-American Danielle Steel."
—Rolling Out

"This one's a page-turner with a very satisfying conclusion."
—RT Book Reviews on SECRET VOWS

Available January 2015 wherever books are sold!

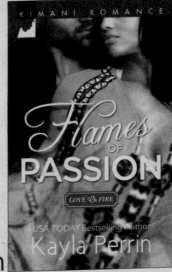

REQUEST YOUR FREE BOOKS!

2 FREE NOVELS
PLUS 2 FREE GIFTS!

KIMANI™
ROMANCE

Love's ultimate destination!

KROM13R

Will her vacation
fling turn into a
forever love?

All of Me

SHERYL LISTER

Declaring a "dating hiatus" was an easy decision for teacher
Karen Morris. She intends to unwind and enjoy a luxurious
Caribbean cruise solo, but businessman Damian Bradshaw
manages to change her mind. They ignite an insatiable need
that neither can deny… Will the promise of a bright future
be enough to rehabilitate their reluctant hearts?

Available January 2015 wherever books are sold!

$$437.31$$
$$-\ 70.26 \text{ (CC)}$$
$$267.05$$
$$-\ 40.01 \text{ (CE)}$$
$$227.04$$
$$-\ 60.00 \text{ (MW)}$$
$$167.04$$